For a... have a story to tell.

2

Mornings are always stressful when Sarah's away.

"Five minutes!" I yell up the stairs, which is met by, "Have you seen my school shoes?"

I groan, knowing the girls will be late for the third time in a row.

Phoebe rushes past me in a blur. "I'm sure they were in the playroom!" she's wailing.

"Where's Lisa?" I ask.

"Why would I know? She's probably still asleep."

"What?"

"Well, I haven't seen her. Did you write me a sick note for PE yet?"

I'd forgotten and I quickly grab a pen, scribbling out the note.

"What do you mean, you haven't seen her?"

Phoebe has now found her shoes and is at the door.

"Dad, we need to go, we're late," she says, leaving the house with her bag over her shoulder.

I grab Lisa's bag and open the car. It's then that I see Lisa's little blonde head peeking out from one of the animal sheds. She always has liked the fact that we live on a farm.

"Lisa!" I bellow and she runs towards us, giggling.

"I was playing with the lambs," she sings merrily.

She has mud up the side of her uniform and I try to brush it off as best I can as I hurry her into the car. The teachers must think them both neglected, arriving at school in the state they do.

"How come Phoebe's in the front? She was in the front yesterday!" Lisa pipes up indignantly as we set off.

"That rule only applies when Mum's driving," Phoebe replies with an air of authority.

To prevent an argument I quickly suggest a round of the song game and both girls are instantly pleased. We spend the rest of the drive making up silly songs to titles I have to come up with. Then we are there and they both disappear with a quick kiss.

When I get back home I have to do the rounds of feeding and cleaning the animals. Although I enjoy this, I mull over the stressful situation I'm in. Currently Sarah is the sole earner due to my art museum closing down unexpectedly, and there are a severely limited number of good jobs out there for a History of Art major.

Once I'm done I return to the house and kick my wellies off. It is only when I'm wiping my feet on the mat that I notice the brown parcel which has been left on the doorstep. I scoop it up, assuming that it must be something Sarah ordered, and I put it next to today's newspaper on the kitchen table. I then put the kettle on in an attempt to convince myself that tea will get me into the right frame of mind to undertake the task of searching through the paper's recruitment section, something which I find both achingly boring and disheartening. It is probably for this reason that once I've made myself comfortable I decide to re-examine the parcel and discover that it has no name on it. I weigh it in my hands and decide the only manly course of action is to ignore my pressing plans and investigate, so I open it.

A weighty book slides on to the table, entitled *Seven Minutes*. I search in vain for an accompanying letter, then open the front cover to see if there is an inscription: there is not. I skim over the first page and I can feel the familiarity of a good book tugging at my mind, making me forget my obligations and offering me an escape. I rock back on my chair, kick my feet up on to the table and begin to read.

* * *

Seven minutes really isn't that long. It's often overlooked by people as an awkward amount of time in which nothing can be achieved. Indeed many groups of seven minutes are spent in people's lives simply waiting. I, however, am a collector and it is my job to make every minute count. Everything can be revealed about a human life in seven minutes. Today has been a particularly interesting collection, as amongst them is the last Mangos.

I often look at my job like a card game – perhaps similar to 'Happy Families' – and I relish collecting full sets.

Today the set has been completed by the life and death of Sabina Mangos.

I sometimes revisit the rest of these preserved lives and watch them intertwine with each other seamlessly again. I turn to the best bits, like one would dog ear a favorite book. Still the people I never knew in life haunt me in their deaths.

She is bent by the side of the river, the evening sun illuminating her cheek bones and her hair is plastered to her face. The memory at first is always startlingly beautiful until the scream begins. It is primal, guttural and echoes off the rocks surrounding her. Then the boy lying limp at her feet comes into focus. But this is my own memory. To understand it better, it's only right that we delve into hers.

ANGELICA: 4.6 minutes

He died with his train ticket in his pocket and his hands clasped tightly around his necklace. I know because I was there. I start compressions frantically, unable to remember how many to do. One, two, three, four, trying to force the life back into him. Five, six, seven, eight, nine, ten, my own breaths rasping, willing him to join me. Eleven, twelve, thirteen, fourteen, I stop pressing methodically, the panic taking over and I begin to hit him wildly. Suddenly I am furious, illogically furious at him, and I begin to spit and swear as I return to compressions. What else can I do?

"Don't die! Wake up! Bastard! Talk to me! Open your eyes now!" I stop suddenly staring rigidly at his face. "No," is all I can think. This. Can't. Happen. Mouth to mouth, my mind screams, I haven't tried that yet and I know why. What if the kiss of life doesn't work; what if it is the kiss of death? What if I can't save him? I slam my hands either side of his head, pinch his nose and calmly breathe into his mouth. Once. Twice. Nothing. And that is when I rock back on to my knees and scream.

***

However, I suppose the story actually begins long before this on the Greek island of Kalymnos. The year is 1917 and, on this particular Thursday, all the local boys are running hectically through the village toward the bay, as they always do as soon as school finishes. And, as always, Mangikas is at the back, struggling to keep up. The other boys had always called him by his surname but he was at the point in his life now where a growing resentment for the name was stirring within him. Water encased him as he plunged in after the others, hugging his knees, staying under for as long as possible in the complete silence, squinting his eyes open against the sting of salt water to see the shafts of sunlight that pierced the blue around him. Then he surfaced and the spell was broken: sound suddenly existed again. Costa splashed his face and another boy shoved his hair over his eyes, forcing him to retaliate by holding him under water in a headlock until someone yelled, "Hey, Mangikas stop trying to be tough, it doesn't suit you."

"Yeah? What does suit me?" he challenged loudly, whilst releasing the boy and gesticulating toward the others.

"Nothing!" Costa joked.

"His name, his name suits him!" There was laughter and general uproar around him which he laughed along with, but his heart clenched with a feeling of loss. His name meant 'the small one'. Not only was this humiliating on many levels and the fuel for many jokes at his expense, but he didn't want it to determine his fate: he did not want to live a small life. He had a big personality and would like to order a life to fit that size. Unfortunately, on Kalymnos life was one size fits all. All those promising youth who splashed in the water would soon be put to work sponge diving, which would eventually damage their lungs beyond repair and they would die painful deaths. The difference on that scorching afternoon was that Mangikas saw he wanted something different.

This was the first important memory his mind gave me on the fateful day where I rushed through his memories to create the collage of his life. At this point I knew nothing of Louise or Angelica or even Clemence. Ah, Clemence. Of course, I knew about him before his time through his mother's memories, and when the time finally came to reveal what became of the rest of his life, I was surprised how few early memories he had. Perhaps he had repressed them.

I first encountered Clemence through his mother's fond gaze when he was only two years old. She herself was a brilliant woman, but underneath her conservatively powdered face was a touch of eccentricity that perhaps her husband brought out. It was clear to everyone that she had desperately wanted her second child to be a girl so I suppose it was unsurprising in her situation with the strains of war, treason on her behalf and her husband's deteriorating health that she felt she deserved to get something she wanted for a change. Whatever the cause, the first time I saw Clemence his already somewhat moody features were obscured by a smudge of blusher on each cheek (not actual blush, due to rationing, but instead the color was achieved through using a needle to prick a finger, draw blood, then apply with a damp tissue), his hair was long with three ribbons tied into it and he was sporting a rather dashing green pinafore which he had dribbled porridge down the front of. Despite the hindrance of his natural messiness, for all intents and purposes he really did look like a little girl. His mother certainly thought so as she fondly stroked his hair. You can just imagine the kind of reaction this got when he had to attend his first day at the Hitler Youth, but that comes later.

But perhaps the life that holds me the most is the one that I have just collected. I could not call it a happy life, but it is one so riddled with mischief that it is one that I love to watch. It is that of the little Sabina who has a problem with injustice, whose mother didn't want her and who has done bad things. It is the story of the little girl who once whizzed down an entire mountain on makeshift skis her uncle had carved and, unable to contain her frenzied joy, flew over a jump, legs and arms spread wide and, unintentionally, yelled "I love life!"

One of the first memories I saved from her I will entitle 'The music lesson', or perhaps 'The question of truth' and I'm sure she must have smiled as she relived this moment for the last time all those years ago in that shabby boarding school.

SABINA: 1.6 minutes

I let my books fall to the ground and slowly bent down to pick them up, trying to waste as much time as possible. Mona appeared from around the corner.

"I'll help," she chimed as she started to gather sheets of paper, apparently in one of her good moods today.

"No, please don't." I snatched the papers off her and slowly rearranged them.

"Why not? You're late again, silly."

I had not told her about my music teacher. In fact, I had not told anyone, even though it plagued me, so I settled on simply glaring at her menacingly to try and communicate that that was the point and also to let her know that she was not yet forgiven for the jelly incident last week.

"Why are you being so snappy?" she snapped.

"Stop being such a moaner, Mona," I retorted, which is pretty much the only thing I have on her but it always annoys her enough to stalk off huffily.

I sigh watching her leave; if I ever want to eat my jelly in peace again, I'm going to have to make it up with her later. I feel a little guilty for the rest of the walk but then my stomach growls and I remember her laughing as she tipped out all my carefully tended pots of jelly that I'd spent hours on the week before, and how excited I'd been to try one, and how I now hadn't eaten properly in three days because the school food was deadly. My self-righteousness returns just as I arrive outside the music room. Gritting my teeth I slowly raise my hand to knock on the door.

Five minutes later I'm subtly shifting away from my music teacher whose green skirted behind is plopped on to the other side of the piano stool. Fixated on the offensive article, I pay little attention to the demonstration of how the introduction to 'Das Albumblatt fur Elise' should be played, but instead keep my hands locked in my lap. I switch my long brown plait to the shoulder furthest away from Mrs. Kruger, lest 'it' should drop. I am woken from my concentration when the unaware Mrs. Kruger instructs me, "Sabina, you must now play that, explaining the notes as you go."

The anxiety in the overheated music room is palpable and, very tentatively, eyes still locked on the droplet of snot hanging at the end of the mistress's nose, I try to play. Mrs. Kruger's nose is like a volcano protruding away from her face; the inside has dried like molten lava, forming a green crust which surrounds the last droplet. It would perhaps have been all right if the mistress had not seemed to insist upon following my hands with her head, making the oncoming threat of rain ever present, and the bobbing motion did not help either. With every new beat I feel that my fingers only narrowly escape the utter foulness of snot from Mrs. Kruger's nose. With all these thoughts on my mind, it is not long before my fingers trip over themselves and the piano protests offensively inducing Mrs. Kruger's cries of, "What is the problem? We have been working on the same piece for weeks! Ignorant girl! Do you never concentrate?"

Her voice is riddled with that utter desperation that only someone who has experienced teaching understands. However, she also has a condescending and self-absorbed demeanor that seems to assume that I am either lazy or stupid. I can still not look away from the droplet which is now only a millimeter away from flying the nest. If I told Mrs. Kruger what was wrong perhaps she would sort it out before next week? Blow her nose before she came to class or something? So, for the first time in the four weeks that I have been trying to learn piano, I meet Mrs. Kruger's eyes. Calmly and quietly, taking a deep breath, I reply, "I'm really sorry but I find it very difficult to concentrate..."

"Why, what's wrong with you?" Mrs. Kruger interrupts.

A little more boldly I answer, "well, every week that I have a lesson, I come and sit here and you always have a drip at the end of your nose that looks like it's about to fall off, and I can't take my eyes of it in case it lands on the piano and touches me!"

I am going to suggest that Mrs. Kruger should blow her nose more frequently but I do not get the opportunity to before her deafening outburst, which includes many repetitions of "I have never been so insulted" and "You spoiled child". She is in the middle of spitting out the word "unappreciative" and looking like she could either cry or hit something, when the drip finally finds itself another home, flying free and landing on the piano.

"See!" I exclaim, having backed away from the oncoming attack, "I told you it would happen.'"

This apparently (though I'd thought it would help her to see reason) is just too much for Mrs. Kruger who grabs hold of my collar and pushes me out of door with the instruction not to bother coming back to piano lessons as she will refuse to teach me and my parents will be informed that they no longer have to pay for them. I catch one last glimpse of Mrs. Kruger's flushed face (whether from anger or embarrassment I don't know) before the door slams in my face. For a moment, staring at the wood inches away from my nose, I feel as if I might cry but instead I sigh, pick up my school bag and walk back towards the dorm. I don't particularly care that my parents will be informed; they probably won't give it a second thought. If it were my gran, I'd have minded a little. But older people are confusing. For example, they're always telling you to tell the truth, don't make up excuses, but then when you obey their laws they get offended! And my parents too, why have a daughter if you're just going to send her off to boarding school?

By the time I enter the dormitory I feel confused. The other ten beds are all empty – everyone is probably still at lunch. I consider going down but I like the escape and besides, yesterday's dinner had been heart and rice, same as every Wednesday, which I never ate. That means they will whip it out again and again until I eat it, in the name of saving money, and I definitely can't stomach that now. Instead I collapse on the bed and think back to more pleasant memories of living with Gran at the boat house to sooth myself.

***

The bizarre part of my job, I suppose, is that I only retrieve and therefore I am only able to view the memories of importance to a specific person. Therefore, in my mind life is disjointed and I ignore the fact that some pieces may not quite fit because it will never be possible for me to be able to review all of the information. I prefer just looking at the highlights anyway. That is not to say that I only retrieve happy memories; it is more that I only retrieve the most prominent. The instant the person dies I must be ready to present their personal seven minutes and it is a skilful job as I am simultaneously organizing and presenting their life. I must confess that I love the challenge – to show each person the value they had, to show them their life before the blackness, and I love to be exposed to each person's experiences. I hoard them and wait expectantly for the deaths of the people who surrounded them so that I can see the story through different eyes and have blanks filled in. Anyway, I fear I may have muddled you at the beginning with the taste of all the lives involved in this particular collection so I have done my best to arrange them in a way which makes sense (and the order, I presume, they go in). I like to cut between each person too. I suppose that's my love of storytelling making me a little showy, but I'll do my best not to indulge in my own dwellings to much... which I am slightly prone to.

Let's go back to the start and the next moment for Mangikas, the young Greek boy.

MANGIKAS: 1.4 minutes

Running away from home was the most daring thing I had ever done. But escape plagued me; I refused to be trapped, to let myself be destroyed.

"Why won't you shut up about that singer, Mangikas?"

"You in love, Mangikas?"

The jibes had been incessant when I'd asked at school but that hadn't stopped me. I could laugh off anything, but I had to know where that singer had come from.

"I didn't realize before, why didn't you tell me I could do something else?"

I'd broached the topic one night over dinner only to receive a cuff on the head accompanied by, "Don't talk with your mouth full!" from my mother. Over-exaggerating my chews until there was no food left in my mouth, I continued, "Papa?"

"What?" Father replied, with his mouth full.

Mother rolled her eyes with a martyr-like "Aye, aye, aye boys!"

"Where did that singer come from?"

"Athens, of course. All of the great singers are Athens born and bred. But you my son, you have the lungs of a deep sea diver! And you should be proud of that!"

Athens was the place to be.

***

I know that I am interrupting the memories, but such is life (excuse the pun). I assure you that I will try to resist the temptation to jump in between each one to give my own opinions and running commentary on the characters, even though my thoughts on each of the human's minutes I think are worthy to share and are very interesting. I just thought I should clarify that our story now moves to Munich in Germany, and though this was not the most prominent of Angelika's memories, I believe it is the earliest one collected.

ANGELICA: 29 seconds

"The war doesn't suit me," I thought glumly as I slowly removed each of the rabbit's ears, trying to hold my breath to prevent my gag reflex. I scowled over at Mother who was humming to herself carelessly and pretending to dust the portrait of Father that hung over the mantelpiece, his wise eyes stared back steadily at me, reminding me to keep my temper.

Slowly I began to skin the rabbit, bitterly thinking that even when we had servants the cooks never had to skin a wild animal. We could afford meat from a real butcher then. With the indignation of realizing that I was now worse than a servant, I threw the knife into the sink and yelled "Get Annabel or Tara to do this. I'm sick of having to look after them because you can't!"

Mother stared for a moment, the way someone marooned on an island stares after the ship, then bent down leaning on her knees so that she was eye level with me.

"My little angel."

I laughed, feeling anything but angelic.

"Your sisters can't do the cooking, they're too young."

"So what's your excuse?" I thought bitterly.

"But I tell you what, your Father's having guests around from the law firm tonight. If you finish the rabbit pie then I'll help you dress up for it with some of my makeup. It would be nice to look pretty, wouldn't it?"

My mother, although partially useless, was an expert at diffusing tension through offerings of fun and eventually vanity won out; I was always transfixed by watching her apply makeup.

When we were finished, I stared at my reflection in the mirror for at least five minutes, tilting my head at different angles to see the effect. I was fascinated by my face. Eventually my mother raised my chin up so I had to look at her instead. She kissed my forehead and said, "You're going to be a heartbreaker one day, my dear." And for the first time since the war broke out, I smiled at her. I liked that very much.

CLEMENCE: 58 seconds

My mother finally let go of my hand when we arrived at the gate and I clenched it a few times to try and get the blood back into it. What was the woman playing at? Theo had come to this place when he was younger, but now was in an older group and she hadn't reacted this way then. A snooty guard said something to her in German which I only half understood.

"They'll get you a uniform inside, my dear," she whispered in my ear, then hugged me too tightly and hurried away.

I stared at the line of other six-year-old boys in front of me. They all looked the same and they all stared straight ahead. The guard steered me to the front of the room, which I instinctively knew was a place I did not want to be.

"Who would like to answer a question?" he roared at the eager crowd.

Everyone's hand shot into the air.

"What does Herr Mangos look like?"

The boys were practically jumping with eagerness to answer, "Herr Reisen."

The blond boy stepped forward, smiling, and yelled, "He looks like a girl, sir!"

I was fairly sure I knew what that meant and I felt my face flush with embarrassment.

"Indeed! And is this what we strive for here at Hitler Youth?"

"No, sir!" everyone chorused.

"Is this the image of the perfect soldier or is this the image of weakness?"

"Weakness, sir!"

"And what happens to the weak?"

"They fall, sir!"

"Gut! Have you got that, Mangos? Let this be a lesson to anyone who thinks they can break the rules, anyone who supports outsiders. Next week you arrive in uniform with your hair cut, do you understand?"

The jeering suddenly ceased and I assumed I was expected to say something. I couldn't understand what the hell they were yelling about so I opted for defiance rather than stupidity and folded my arms slowly across my chest to make it look like I was choosing not to answer. This turned out to be a very bad idea as the guard smacked me hard across the cheek, sending me to the floor where I hit the same cheek again and, much to my embarrassment, I cried out in pain. I prised my eyes open to try and find some reassurance but my vision was blocked by the jeering faces of my 'classmates'. Then I was hauled to my feet again and my audience clapped as the guard removed his belt and struck me across the back with it. He stopped me falling forward by shoving a uniform into my hands.

"Now you will go and put your uniform on."

I hobbled to the corner with gritted teeth, hating humanity, hating myself and, most of all, hating my mother.

The rest of the session was horrible, every command I did was late because I couldn't understand what was being asked of me. I was isolated, the outcast, and this, as my walk home proved, meant I would not be safe. Five boys my age circled me.

"Do you actually have a ribbon in your hair?" one jeered.

In order to prevent another misunderstanding, I decided to come clean.

"I don't understand you."

"Speak in German, you filth!"

"I don't think he can."

"You don't speak German?" one of them asked in utter disbelief.

"I speak a little, my... my parents speak to us in English though."

"Then your parents are traitors."

"No, they're not."

"And what are you? Are you a boy or a girl or just plain dirt?"

"What's this?" One of them tugged at my shoulder-length hair. "Did you want to look pretty for your first day of school?"

I recognized this as a threat and decided my best option was to run. Unfortunately, this presented them with the prospect of a chase, and because people are cruel they pursued me. One of them started throwing rocks and all the while they were yelling and laughing. Although many missed me, some hit the cut in my back the belt had already made which was so excruciating I was amazed my legs kept functioning. They kept me going until I realized I was lost and with that I knew what was coming; rocks hit me from all sides and then the kicks and punches began. I had never even had a bruise before and now I wouldn't be seeing my actual skin color for weeks. The pain was only kept at bay by the fear; I didn't want to die, not now and not like this, begging and wailing like the worthless being I was. For a moment anger rushed up through me, pure and clear and as hot metal, but it was dislodged by a kick to the nose which ripped my head back. With that I lost all bodily control and I felt the snow around me warm slightly as I wet myself lying face down in the street. Eventually the laughter faded and I was left alone – lost and surrounded in my own filth. Hatred was all I could feel.

* * *

I shut the book hurriedly, having completely forgotten the time. I'm already twenty minutes late to pick the girls up and I haven't done any job searching. I reprimand myself and hurry out, thinking of the lives of the people I have just been absorbed with. I'm also not quite sure what I have read, though the time clearly flew by. The people aren't quite clear to me yet, but little Sabina's 'memory' was entertaining enough to make me want to hear more of her story, and Clemence too.

I force myself to think in the present as my girls come running up to the car. After I have made dinner and helped the girls with their homework, I am thoroughly looking forward to my wife's return tomorrow. Single father duties do not come naturally to me and I am relieved when the house is finally quiet and I can curl up in bed and continue to read.

* * *

SABINA: 40 seconds

"Deckel hoch der kessel kocht."

I would hear that phrase in my sleep and dread the inevitable walk to the Kinder Garten. Once again I have to resist the urge to ask my Gran to escort me from the boats house to my school. My boots crunch reassuringly on the fresh snow beneath me as I walk, clutching my satchel and trying to appear the image of nonchalance. I stride past the shops, knowing I'm safe with the shopkeepers smiling down at me from their windows. The baker's boy, Klaus, even waves at me and I try not to smile too widely in return.

My moment of glee comes to an untimely end as I hear the footsteps behind me. I know I have to turn the corner in a couple of strides and then no one will be able to see me. Three strides left. I am overcome by the usual tooth-crumbling fear as I break into a jog but one of them grabs my satchel, pulling me backwards and laughing at my pathetic escape attempt. He is a full head taller than me and his skin looks like the inside of an old tea pot. The other two catch up and pinch my arms while I yell abuse. Then, as always, all three grab my school skirt and wrench in up over my head so my knickers are on show to the entire world. As I run away to the safety of school, I hear the chant, "Deckel hoch der kessel kocht," (lift up the lid the kettle's boiling), and it rings in my head long after I'm out of reach. Cruel and pointless and threatening, I hate boys! It is not until I reach my first class that I realize they still have my satchel and I have to lie and say I forgot it, for which I get a stern telling off at the front of the class.

It's a Friday, which means fish for tea, and the entire time Gran cooks she merrily shares stories of her day with me, not many of which I follow in their entirety. I zone out distractedly until she presents me with a fresh loaf, which her friend the baker gave her for a discounted rate with a wink and a conspiratorial "For my favorite customer." I think I almost see her blush at this point. She pauses for the first time since picking me up and asks me about my homework.

"It's Friday Gran, I'm not thinking about that yet," I cover quickly.

She chuckles quietly. "I know the feeling dear."

I smile relieved, but she continues, "Still everything's better if you face it. Let's see how much you have to do so we can plan are weekend around that. Where's your homework diary?"

I start to panic and testily reply, "I said I don't want to think about it tonight!"

"Bini, what's the problem? I just want to see."

"You don't understand. I won't give it to you."

"You won't give it to me?"

"No!" I'm almost yelling now.

"Sabina, why won't you give me that diary?"

I crack and feel hot tears of embarrassment rolling down my cheeks. I look down, biting my lip and trying to sound calm, I say, "I can't."

Gran stares at me bemused and concerned. I suddenly throw myself into her arms and sob uncontrollably. "I can't give it to you because I don't have it!"

Slowly over a mug of steaming chamomile tea (her cure for everything from a stomach ache to a bad mood) and the smell of sizzling fish, I confess the entire story. Luckily for me my Gran doesn't go in for complaining to authorities and thinking that will solve the issue, as so many grownups are conned into believing. Instead she communicates with me on a level that appeals far more: revenge.

"We need a plan, Bini, that's all. Something that'll teach them a lesson." I nod enthusiastically. "Lucky for you I have some powerful friends. I am, after all, Mr. Ries's favorite customer," she winks.

"Please don't tell him about this!" I beg, distressed.

"I'm going to have to if he's going to help us, but don't be embarrassed, this isn't your fault!"

Gran walks me to school on Monday and en route we stop in at the bakery where I am momentarily dazed by the onslaught of delicious smells that surround me. For a moment I truly believe that I have walked into heaven. The scene before me comes sharply back into focus as Mr. Reis's usually jovial face is distorted by a frown and he gruffly remarks, "They what?"

I stare sheepishly at my feet and knock some of the snow off the toe of my boot to look inconspicuous. At that moment Mr. Reis's anger is mirrored by his son's, who storms into the front of the shop with a look of disgust.

"We'll show those little hooligans a thing or two."

I glance up in time to meet his eyes and see pity there and I know that they will both take part in the plan.

The next morning I walk to school, seemingly alone, and soon hear the following footsteps. I smile quietly to myself in anticipation and before the turning, I slip through a gap in the hedge and crouch down in front of the pile of pre-made, stone-filled snowballs with the baker, his son and Gran. Peering through the hedge I can see the three boys, looking puzzled, but then they begin to tease. "Little Sabina… you can't hide forever."

And then the expected "Deckel hoch der kessel...", but this time the oldest one didn't get to finish his chant. The baker's boy pops his head over the hedge and launches the first attack; the snow shatters around the boy's face and he clutches his nose where the rock has clearly hit.

"Leave Sabina alone or you will have to face me," he bellows and the other three of us pop up immediately and begin to lob the rest of the stone-balls at them as they frantically, and with comic terror, begin to run away. After a few seconds I can't contain it anymore and I begin to laugh wholeheartedly at their clown-like shock. I look over to see the other three enjoying it almost as much as me; I guess everyone likes to see justice.

"Good riddance!" Gran bellows as they disappear down the final street.

I know that they will never give me trouble again and I can't help thinking that I have the coolest Gran in the world. The baker's son, Klaus, is brushing the snow from his hands on his jeans and stating, "That'll teach them." In a moment of impulse I kiss him on the cheek, a thank you kiss I suppose. I know I've said I hate boys, but maybe not all boys.

MANGIKAS: 2.8 minutes

"Athens." I tasted the word in my mouth. I sang it, breathed it in with my new freedom. This was love as far as I was concerned; the dust, the bustle, the laughter. Athens was the place to be, and it welcomed me like an embrace. I knew things would work for me here. The best school in the city had accepted me on a singing scholarship.

"Can you sing?" a snooty teacher had enquired.

"Of course, practically professional," I had grinned in reply, not guessing that they would put me to the test immediately, but when things are meant to work, they do.

Singing was like that moment of stillness underwater – utter peace and clarity. I had discovered my second love. Hmm, that's 1. Athens, 2. Singing, I needed to leave room for my love of food as well. At this rate how would there ever be room for me to love a woman? My heart was full!

After I had finished the song, she had smiled slightly.

"What is your name, boy?"

I recognized at that moment the opportunity I was being given. God must have realized he had overlooked me when he dumped me on Kalymnos, and now he was allowing me a fresh start. This must be what they mean when they talk of being 'born again'. I would no longer be Mangikos, the small one, no. I altered it quickly to Mangos.

"Well, Mr. Mangos, your voice needs training for sure, but we would be very happy to accept you with a full scholarship."

I knew I was a natural and I grinned at her affirmation of my talent. Life would now be mine and I think this outlook was a kind of magnet as, by the end of my first day, I was the center of a large group of boys who were transfixed by my history. Mangos, abandoned on an island at birth, who tamed wild snakes and learnt to sing by imitating the birds. No one mocked me; the eyes I met were not filled with doubt but with acceptance, and I looked forward to tomorrow for the first time in years. I'm sure there were doubters but I was an unstoppable force and anyone who thought I was lying thought it was damn funny, so I couldn't lose.

After a month the initial triumph wore off and I could no longer pass off that pang of guilt as indigestion so I bought a postcard to write home on. I labored over what to say for an hour, yelling at anyone who tried to come into my room. Eventually I settled for the truth as eloquently as I could muster.

'Mum and Dad, I know you will never forgive me for running away. You won't understand why but I can tell you it was so I will live! Have joined opera college, very happy. I don't train the hardest but I am the best. Don't worry about marriage or anything, I'll soon get famous (a touring opera company has been interested in my voice already!) and then that won't be a problem. I'll visit, yours Mangos (formerly Mangikas)'

***

Human behavior never ceases to fascinate me – why we like one person more than another, for example. It's odd. If we are all just bodies with the same potential as each other – the ability to jump, be creative, lie, fall in love. So is it merely how we do those things that makes us more accessible to one person and not another. If a soul exists, is that it? The how? I admit I have nothing to do with the 'after' part. That is another department entirely, and indeed I do not know if such a department even exists. There is a death department, which I am not involved in. I prefer to focus on the value of life, even if it is in the past; to me that does not decrease its value. If anything, I think it increases it. It's now the finished product, done. What happened, happened, and it is how it stays. Of course, I can't take human form anymore but if I could, I would imagine myself as a grey professor who wears checked shirts and makes enthusiastic hand gestures.

But I prefer watching the lives of others, rather than living myself, and as I re-watch these people a sense of nostalgia is overtaking me. I will miss this job, but I know it cannot be my time much longer and so I savor this last collection.

ANGELICA: 58 seconds

I had that recurring nightmare again last night. I'm in a dank cave and there is a massive stone slab in front of me and a lever in the corner. All at once the lever is pulled down by an invisible force and the slab rotates slowly, revealing two people frozen in a block of ice.

They are always people I know and I must decide which one is allowed to live. The first pair is Annabelle, my little sister, still clutching her teddy, and the other Mrs. Houn from school. Although I quite like Mrs. Houn, there is no competition and I instantly point to Annabelle who runs free and hugs me, looking confused. As always I have to explain that I have just chosen her life over the other. She then stands behind me, as all the others will, to watch my subsequent choices.

The combinations are sometimes easy and sometimes heart-wrenching, such as when the block contains my dad and my other sister and I begin to cry. I don't know who to choose. I try to pull the lever by hand, to skip this choice, but it is too stiff. I bang on the ice, yell, curse, but no one reacts. Defeated I slowly point to my dad; he walks free looking concerned. "Angel, what's going on?" How can I tell him that I have just let one of his children die? I can't; he'll hate me. And what about little Tara? What about her life? I wake up screaming.

"Hey Angel, shh, just a dream my love."

I'm wrapped in my father's strong arms and I can smell the inky and wood-like smell I associate with him and I cry into his shoulder unashamedly.

"You want to tell me what happened?" he asks when I calm down enough to breath.

I shake my head quickly. He nods like he understands and also like he's talking to a grown up, which I like.

"Well, Daddy's still got some work to do. Would you like to help?"

Soon I am tucked into his big work chair with a blanket around me and I begin to relax.

"It's like I'm the manager," I say.

Dad quickly jumps backwards with a "Yes sir!" He salutes and I laugh.

I help with sorting out some files while he continues writing out cases or something for his law firm. I could watch my dad work for hours. He has total focus on what he is doing, although he has been looking increasingly tired recently and, as I watch him, he removes his glasses and rubs his eyes.

"You look old," I say sincerely, and he looks at me and laughs.

When other people laugh it usually makes me feel a little dead inside, but not when Dad laughs. He only laughs when it is genuine, not like my mother who laughs at anything, so if I make my Dad laugh I feel a sense of achievement.

"Do I now? Well, I'm not that past it yet missy, I can still do this," and he artfully tickles me until I can't help but snort with laughter. I also no longer mind being silly if I'm around my dad, probably because I know he works so hard that I feel like he earns his fun moments. He ruffles my hair and goes back to his desk and I watch him work serenely until I fall in to a dreamless sleep.

I like school, I'm the best in my class easily and my teachers like me. Some of the other children don't because they see me as a threat, or at least that's what my dad said when I told him about the teasing.

"There's nothing more dangerous than someone who can work hard. It makes people jealous because there is nothing you can't achieve with hard work."

I took this very seriously and so I work hard. The worst of the teasing is from an insufferable boy called Hannis who sits behind me and constantly tugs on my plait, making the other boys snicker as he whispers "know it all" under his breath. I resolutely ignore him and his stupid side parting. This gets more difficult, however, on the walk home where there is nothing else to focus on. Today he ran up behind me and tugged my plait by way of greeting; personally I see nothing wrong with a traditional "hello".

"Know it all!"

Ignore it.

"Know it all," He makes it into a song now and blasts it out tunelessly

"Stop it!"

He grins triumphantly. "Made you talk to me""

I storm away but he overtakes me and jogs backwards in front of me. "Anyway, I was just told to warn you."

"Warn me about what?"

"About what happens to teachers' pets."

I sigh. "I don't care Hannis, I really don't care."

"Fine, but you should know anyway. It's happened to loads of teachers' pet's already...'"

He waits for my reaction but I don't give him the satisfaction.

"At night a mad scientist climbs in through their windows and steals their brains."

I stop. "That's not true."

"Whatever, but I bet you'll close your window tonight!"

I'm stonily silent after that until he puts his hand in mine.

"What are you doing?" I yell, pulling free.

"Can I walk you home?"

"No!"

"Come on Angie, we both know you secretly want me to walk you home... and hold your hand... and..."

"Shut up Hannis!" I push him aside and storm ahead furiously.

"Angie, wait, wait, I'll give you a challenge."

I pause. He knows he's caught my interest by appealing to my competitive side.

"What sort of challenge?"

It will be fun to watch the smug smile slide off his face when he loses.

"Well, what are you good at?"

I grin. "Everything."

"All right. If I win I get to walk you home… deal?"

The task is to climb over the highest fence in the village and pilfer apples from a large and laden tree that sits just behind Mrs. Samsel's tiny rundown house. None of the children have ever seen her leave and there is a rumor that she is a practicing witch or, worse, a spy. There is one large lit window that faces directly at the fence and I scan for the least conspicuous route round the house while Hannis finalizes the rules.

"So we each have to get two apples back over the fence and not be seen or get caught, and the first person to drop their apples…" he shrugs his backpack off his shoulders and takes three elaborate paces from the fence before carefully marking the spot, "there, wins the challenge."

He smiles at me crookedly. "Ready steady go!" he suddenly shouts in one breath, and without warning, so that he has started on the fence before I can even set off.

I storm after him, furious and I climb the fence with an instinctive ferocity. We reach the trees at roughly the same time and I snatch the nearest two apples off a branch. Skimming back behind the house on the side opposite the window, I reach the fence, frantically throwing the apples over before climbing and it is then that I hear the cry. I glance back to see that Hannis has tripped up and is hurriedly chasing down one of his apples which lures him straight into the path of the terrifying Mrs. Samsel. I leap the fence hurriedly and place my apples on top of his rucksack then hang around to watch the rest of the scene, feeling thoroughly pleased and entertained. I smirk the whole way home thinking of his terrified face as she dangled him by his collar and smacked his behind with her door mat.

Sitting on my bed later, I begin to worry. If there are actually mad scientists out there I think my brain would be one of the ones they'd want; it is pretty good. I sleep with the window shut that night.

LOUISE: 6.4 minutes

My heart was throwing itself manically against my chest the entire time. It clearly wanted no part in this crazy endeavor that could have deathly consequences. I'd taken two taxis and gone two miles out of the way, just like I had been instructed to do. Why did I agree to this? After so long of trying to keep my head down and keep my family safe... Safe, that's an interesting word, isn't it. The 'f' peaks over the rest of the word inquisitively, as if already trying to defy the meaning of the word it's been placed in. Stop it Lou, I always do this to distract myself, focus on language and words rather than the situation at hand.

I walk along the cold, bland corridor and see myself reflected in the full length mirror at the end. I've always thought I look a little like a question mark, my head and shoulders are at a constant tilt and my face's default expression is quizzical. If I'm taking this literally, I suppose my little black-clad feet portray the full stop fairly well too. So many questions. I'm always questioning. Will the children be ok? How soon will Stefanos die? How will I cope when I'm alone? Should I even be here?

I bite the inside of my cheek; it's just a job like any other. I push open the door and, as instructed, there are a group of soldiers waiting silently for me to begin. I see the determination on their faces and I know that this is not just a job, this is not just for my family: this is for my country.

* * *

God, it's one in the morning and I only know this because my eyes have become so blurry that I can't read the next section now. I've never been one for late nights, I don't get anything out of them. I let the book fall to the floor, dimly hoping that I've marked where I was to save the aggravation of trying to re-find my place, as, awkwardly, it doesn't have a table of contents or, for that matter, chapters as such which is slightly frustrating.

Sleep! I need to be rested for my wife's homecoming tomorrow, well, today now actually. I try picturing sun and wine and other things that make me feel sleepy.

So, Louise is alive in some kind of war. I wonder if it's the First or Second World War. Imagine spying for your country... I wonder if I'd have had the courage to do that? Ok mind, please stop. I need to sleep. Now.

After ten minutes of my mind messing me around, I give up, roll over and rummage for the book. Yes the page is marked – I inwardly congratulate my past self's presence of mind – and then I lie back and focus my mind on the lives of others.

* * *

CLEMENCE: 1.2 minutes

I roll the cigarette, like my father used to. I love the texture between fingers, the familiarity it holds and the promise of peace soon. I inhale deeply as I lean back against the shed. Why should I care? I don't even like the woman much. I turn suddenly and hit the shed hard with my fist to try and get rid of the anger pulsing through me. I slide down the shed slowly, inhaling again and closing my eyes.

"Hey, little brother."

Oh God, not now. I swear I'm going to rip him to shreds this time.

"Beating up things that can't fight back again? Scared you're going to lose?"

I get up, counting backwards from ten as I've learnt to do to stop myself from acting on violent impulses, and manage to reply quietly, "You may be head of whatever goddamn Nazi army shit, but that's all over now, Theo, you have nothing. And you may still be taller, but you sure as hell aren't stronger, so don't piss me off."

It's true, my hate of the Germans has meant that I've had to gain muscle over the years. I can now speak fluent German but it still leaves a nasty taste in my mouth. Theo took to the whole set up; come on, it was in his name "Theo", like a bloody Greek god or something. And didn't everyone think that – athlete, success – and then Clemence, weedy, failure, known as "the odd one" by almost everyone at school. Because I have my own opinions and I'm not a lapdog, like Theo, that didn't stop him bullying the shit out of me when we were younger to prove his loyalty to them and not me.

"Woah, calm down, we need to talk about who's going to go with Mum."

"To England? Theo, why the hell would I go to England? There's nothing there for me."

"Well, one of us should go with her. I mean you know we owe it to her; she raised us and she wants to go home, now she can."

"So bugger off then."

"Listen, I have a life here. I'm well respected, but you've got shit all!" He laughs boomingly and nudges me provokingly. I want to kill him.

"Bloody clever, aren't you, make me feel shit, play the brother card – 'You owe it to her'. I don't owe any one anything! I'm going to show you all, I'm going to be rich and happy while you march around like a muppet."

"Don't be bloody stupid, where the hell are you going to get a job? You're stupid… You know you're going to kill yourself on those things just like Dad did."

And with that encouraging parting comment, I throw my cigarette butt at him, turn on my heel, pack a bag and hop on the first train that arrives at the station. I have a thousand Reichsmark in my pocket, only some of which is stolen. I lean back in my seat watching the streets of people enjoying new-found safety and dealing with the repercussions of war, my head begins to clear. The whole thing was stupid, in my opinion anyway, and that makes me smart. I light another cigarette, musing over what to do now. God, what to do with the rest of my goddamn life. I guess it would be normal to be sad, to have so little holding you to a place that you can just up and leave, but it doesn't. It makes me feel free. Maybe it's genetic, after all my dad did the same thing when he was sixteen, just two years younger than I am now. I don't blame him for wanting to escape from Greece where there's nothing for sale, no access…

Hmm this could be perfect. God, how ironic that the very place my dad hated could be the key to making money. Now is the perfect time for business as everyone's trying to rebuild themselves. I blow the cigarette smoke in circles in front of me and an elderly woman coughs pointedly from the next seat, like it can even reach her from here. Jesus, calm down darling, the war's over, try and smile a little. You probably won't live that much longer anyway. I slowly stub out the cigarette and count backwards from ten again with gritted teeth.

I get off at the next stop before the train's fully halted, throwing my rucksack off first. I light up another cigarette; my stock's running low and I've made myself swear not to buy anything until I've earned my first pay check. I set off down the road, trying not to resign myself to the fact that everyone else could have been right. What if I am stupid? I'm not, though. I got good grades and I speak bloody Greek, German and English! But as I pass through three towns, finding nothing that appeals and being shunned by three café jobs, I start to wonder if Theo made some sense. I don't suppose I'm attractive. He got our mother's blue eyes and he's blond, while I got our father's dark shock of hair and olive skin. And I'm not exactly likeable, in fact I'm not sure anyone has ever liked me. I chuckle darkly to myself as I sit on my bag for a rest in a car park, thinking that bodes well.

"Oi, lad you can't sit here."

For the love of God, will no one cut me some slack? It's not worth the fight so I unclench my fist and pick my bag back up, counting back from ten. At five I decide to try something and I use Theo's interested and flattering voice, "Say, what is this place, do you own it sir?"

Sickening, sickening, sickening.

"Well actually laddy, I do."

Laddy, who in hell calls people that?

"So it's your business then?"

"Yeah, my business is checking cars, you know, road-worthiness." I nod as if I'm captivated while secretly thinking that "worthiness" is probably the longest word this man knows.

"But this lot here," he gestures to our surroundings, "None of them have got a TUV, they're gonna be scrapped some time."

I stared at the rows of cars and smiled. "How much would you give me one for?"

That may have been a bit too gruff so I quickly add, "Sorry, I'm desperate, my old man died recently and I have to help my sick mother."

I see the man's ruddy face soften. God I'm good at this; see, I can be likeable when I need to be.

"Kid, you know these old bangers won't last long, right?"

"Yeh, I get that." I'm not as dense as you. "I guess something's better than nothing though right? And it's all I can afford."

"How much you got?"

"Only 700 Reichsmark." He eyes me doubtfully so I quickly add, "and two packets of cigarettes." I've been around enough to know that you can get almost anything in exchange for good cigarettes nowadays.

He looks me up and down. "These times eh?"

I laugh amiably, "Yeah, yeah."

"Look, you seem like a good kid... aww hell, which one do ya want?"

I've had my eye on a tough looking old car that has a white roof and red sides, even if the paint is peeling off it looks like it can do the job. Within five minutes the deal is done. I spend all night cleaning it at a gas station until it literally looks like new and by seven a.m. I'm on the road, making the trip my dad once took us on to visit his parents in Greece, window down, cigarette in hand. It's a free world now and I'm a free man, it's anyone's game.

The language I use at the different borders varies depending on how they fared in the war, and by the time I reach Greece I praise God that I have a Greek passport. The security guard bangs on the window angrily. I roll it down and am immediately attacked with a vicious "Where are you from?" I can see his hand clutched tightly round his gun. "Answer me, are you from Germany?"

"No, no I'm English, but I have family in Greece. My dad was Greek," the man's stance relaxes

"Oh," He grunts "sorry to scare you, you won't believe the amount of arrogant sons of bithches we've had trying to come over here, like nothing ever happened. War's over, forgive and forget. Yeah well, I got family, you know what I mean?"

He continues to grumble as he checks over my passport and finally I'm through.

I have the product. I just need a buyer, and this thing's not going to hold out much longer so it better be fast. I single out the biggest shop I can find and decide to target it.

Ducking under the shell-clad entrance, I roll up my sleeves due to the heat that I'm not used to. I'm unsure how to negotiate this sale; if it's some guy who figures me for a fraud this whole thing is going to hit the shits. Oh God, it's worse; a pretty Greek girl stands behind the counter counting change. Girls have always avoided my like the plague, so she probably won't even let me speak. I run my hand through my hair and duck behind the nearest shelf to try and get a grip on a lifetime of insecurity. Just say it, product and buyer, she won't humiliate you. What's the worst that can happen? She doesn't buy the car. Ok, I can cope with that.

I shake my hands out, get a grip, I walk towards the counter slowly and she looks up.

"Can I help you?"

Well, that's not entirely how I wanted the conversation to start. Now she's in charge. Wait, I can save this. I answer her in Greek.

"Actually, I was thinking I could help you."

I must look ridiculous I'm staring mostly at the floor and my voice is low due to mumbling shyness,

"Oh really?" The girl raises her eyebrows with a smile. "And how would you do that?"

I tap the counter with my hand nervously. "Well, you see I have this car I need to sell."

"Are you Greek?" she interrupts.

This throws me off. Why would she want to know this?

I hesitate, "Half Greek, half English."

"Yes, I thought so, you look quite Greek but you talk with a nice accent."

I stare at her blankly.

"Sorry," she continues. "I just noticed,"' and she blushes.

Am I making her nervous? I test this new theory tentatively to see how much power I actually hold.

"That's very intuitive of you."

She laughs. This is brilliant.

I reach over the counter and lightly touch her hand. "Yeah, so I have this car. It's my boss's and he's made me drive from Yugoslavia to Greece to sell it. Brand new car and an absolute necessity to any upcoming business, like this fine place that you seem to be running here."

Her eyes are wide and understanding, so I decide to elaborate. "You see, my dad recently died, so I had to get this job to support the rest of my family. I really need someone to buy this car from me."

She has punctuated my spiel with appropriate "oh's" and is now staring at me tragically.

"God, I can't imagine how hard that must be for you. Yes, please show me the car."

I sell it for a healthy amount and stash my victory money in my back pocket in triumph. This is going to work.

I'm turning to leave when I hear my name. I turn quizzically, thinking she must've found something wrong with the car, but she's looking at me.

"Um, it was nice to meet you."

Ok, sure.

"It's always good to meet a nice girl."

She bites her lip, staring at me until it's unnerving.

"Well, bye then."

"You had a long drive, right?"

Oh God, here comes the inquiry. "Yep, but nothing that the car couldn't handle."

"No," she giggles, "that's not what I meant. It's just... would you like to stay for dinner?"

Is this an invitation? Maybe I am attractive to women, just not the stuck up, brain washed ones I went to school with. A smile cracks across my face; I never thought anyone would find me good looking.

"I'd like that very much."

After a bottle of wine she is on my lap, spilling her entire history – arranged marriage to a man she couldn't stand, young widow, inherited this business, frowned on by her family for not having children. She stares at me imploringly with watery brown eyes, her hips touching mine, her breasts pushed against my chest. I don't know what to say. I want this woman. The only people I've ever seen being romantic were my mum and dad so I say what my dad always used to.

"You have beautiful eyes."

And with that, I'm in.

The next morning I catch the train back home, sitting with the wind blowing across my face, the sun warming my skin and the taste of Lilah's kisses from the night before. Utter euphoria. I rejoice in my new found discovery: sex. I love women. They're gentle and reactive to touch and words. Men are aggressive or stupid, or both. Who'd have thought? Clemence Mangos, no longer a virgin. Ha, I think I even beat my brother, brilliant.

Utterly satisfied I light a cigarette and gloat over the best night of my life, my new-found money making skills and my good looks. And I have to smile. What can't I do?

* * *

I read almost all night and I'm not entirely sure why. Even this morning I hurried through sending job applications in order to squeeze in more reading time. I blame it on the need for an outlet; without work I'll be lost, so maybe this is my way of not facing that. Besides, there is something in me that connects with these characters and something about them that I instantly recognize. I want to know more about this self-named 'collector' too. I sort of warm to him. However, about an hour before Sarah's due back I resist the lure of the future pages and focus on getting ready. I like to dress up a bit if she's been away for a while and I sort out the kids so that she can just enjoy them welcoming her home. I don't know why, but I also hide the book at the back of the bookshelf behind an old art history book that no one else would pick up to read.

It is a relief to see her and to have dinner, all four of us together. Everything seems easier when she's around; the conversation, tasks, being in a good mood. Lisa once picked up on this saying that she liked me better when Mummy was around and I had to agree.

We all turn in early after Sarah's surprised the girls with some little gifts she's bought back – a small perfume each from the duty free and some real German chocolates. They are thrilled and decide to both dress up and wear the perfumes tomorrow when we go for lunch at Anne's house.

"Where's my gift?" I jokingly protest.

"Later," she smiles taking my hand.

Afterwards, as we lie in bed together, I hold her close to me.

"Are you ok?"

She sighs and smiles. "Working for my goddamn mother hasn't killed me yet, if that's what you mean."

I laugh, then stop. I was about to ask her how many times I'd told her to quit, but I don't want to suggest that as right now we both know it's not an option. So I stroke her hair soothingly until gradually we both fall asleep.

Somehow Sarah gets us out the door on time and the car is filled with the waft of perfumes from the back. The girls have overdone it a bit and I roll my eyes at Sarah, who laughs, but neither of us want to kill there buzz so we don't comment on it. Anne was one of Sarah's friends from university who has now married an

American and who we have to visit every eight weeks or so. The two women catch up in the kitchen while I am forced to make awkwardly polite conversation with her husband, whose name I am trying to remember. To my relief his phone goes and he leaves, saying that he has to take it as it is business.

I walk over to the window and watch the girls playing an elaborate game in the garden, jumping of the benches determinedly. I wonder what world they're in as they are certainly not here with me. My eyes wander to the black and white pictures on the wall which have been passed down and I am instantly captivated. Hungrily I study each one of them. I've always loved old photos – the stories from another time, people who have long gone but whose stories live on in frozen moments. It makes me think of the book I'm reading at the moment and a part of me wishes that the people I'm learning about were real once, and that I could see them in frozen moments like the ones I'm staring at now. Greedily I also wish that each of the pictures hanging on the wall had a back story attached to tell me who was this person, what color did they like, who did they love, what were their thoughts when the picture was taken? But these, sadly, are lost to me.

At lunch the food is far more enjoyable then the conversation, which mainly centers on our hosts quizzing me on my current unemployment. Sarah reaches out and grips my hand under the table reassuringly and we leave early, laughing it off on the way home. That night, once everyone else is asleep, I retrieve the book and open it from where I left off.

* * *

SABINA: 49 Seconds

This summer was the longest summer I had ever experienced. I hated my mother for bringing me back. I crumpled up the little note left for me in the empty house and added it to the pile. The message was always similar: 'Sabina, guests tonight, need dinner ready by 7, could you clean the lounge and organize book shelf too, Mum.' That was a joke, 'Mum'. I had never called her that. I call my grandma Mum; my home is with her and Lady. I sigh as a shuffle along to the kitchen to find a cook book. Why do I do it? How many times have I resolved to escape, pack a bag and find my home again or even find my real dad? Although I hate to admit it, I know the answer; even though I can't stand her, I want her to like me. Why doesn't she? What's wrong with me? On some disturbing level I have this optimistic idea that this is a test of my loyalty and if I complete all of the lists, she will come home, turn to me smiling then hug me and say "I'm sorry darling, I've missed you so much! Things will be better now, it's me and you."

Of course this never actually happens, and as I watch the water coming to the boil I begin to think she's realizing her mistake. She can't care for me… or she won't probably because I'm an abomination, or because of my history as a psychopathic evil spirit with a vengeance. Why does she hate me so much? And I literally think she does. I am forbidden to leave the house except for school, the phones are all robbed of their batteries when I am around in case I contact someone. And say what? "Hello, person I have never met before, just to let you know I hate my mum, and p.s. my step-dad's a raging alcoholic. Have a nice day, bye." Yes that's very likely.

I know why I'm here though, and it's my fault. If it wasn't for that I'd still be with Gran, swimming in the lake every morning and following the ducks through the reeds, or dressing up Lady in my old bonnets. She's the biggest dog I have ever seen with thick fur and an endlessly trusting face. She would follow me around everywhere and whimper when I left for school in the morning. Boldly I would ride my noble steed into the unknown waters while Gran would narrate the story and Lady would stand proud and calm as I made reins for her and we saved the world.

The day my mum decided she would pick me up from school, I was warned by my Gran in the morning over breakfast and I pleaded with her to come too. I remember fretting over it all day, unable to concentrate in my lessons. There had to be a way out of this and gradually I tried to construct a plan. My great escape consisted of hiding in a tree as soon as the school bell went so she couldn't find me. I was halfway up when I heard her voice and I climbed faster and higher until the leaves obscured me from view completely. I settled down between two branches, clutching my rucksack, knowing it would be a fair wait. Once I was comfortable I felt a quiet smile of triumph break over my face, knowing the annoyance this would cause her. Eventually I heard her over-exaggerated stress, "Where is she then?" and I had to cover my hand with my mouth to stifle a laugh of victory. Gran then joined her. "Perhaps she didn't want to see you…" Well said, Gran!

Unfortunately my mother did not understand subtleties and loudly voiced her self-absorbed indignation. "Of course she wants to see me, I'm her mother." Then the yelling began, "Sabina, Sabina! I know you can hear me!" It got increasingly angry. "What are you playing at?" And then, like all tactical mothers, she decided to get the teaching staff involved and so a pathetic search party was traipsing round the small park by the school calling my name. I couldn't possibly show myself after that; I had to face these teachers every day and they would think I was selfish and melodramatic because they wouldn't bother to find out the whole story. So I stayed put until Gran suggested I may be at home and the search was called off, but not before I heard my mother turn to Gran questioningly, "Home?" They were almost right below my tree now. "What on earth do you mean by home, Mother? She is my daughter and I don't know what you're trying to do, filling her head with stupid stories. Are you trying to take her? I'm not going to have it, you couldn't look after us. I looked after everyone and now you're trying to make up for that by acting like a hero. Well, I'm not having it."

And with that she stomped of bellowing more threats combined with my name. I sat stunned for a while watching the people in the park from where I sat. It had been a long day of worrying (a very draining past-time). I leant back so my face was in the sun and as the yells faded, I allowed myself to exhale and close my eyes.

Heart in my throat and air all around me, I flung my arms out widely trying to catch myself on something and stop this. My mind raced and I cursed myself for my own stupidity. I remember thinking that only I could be dumb enough to be the cause of my own death by falling asleep in a tree. Then pain consumed me.

When I woke up I was in my room at my mother's with a cast on my arm and a note on the table next to me in an otherwise empty house.

I did not see my mother the next day and tried to complete her set chores awkwardly with one arm. I am fairly sure that this new arrangement is permanent and I am desperate to find my Gran to say goodbye but I have no way of doing this.

Before I fell asleep that night, and as my mind sorted through everything I am, my one demand to the universe or God or fate was to stop the world so I could get off. I felt tears warm my cheek with the knowledge that this was not possible. I was woken by a pain in my cheeks so startling that I screamed out. My hands shot up to my face to find the source of the pain and I screamed again. My face was totally alien to me. Shakily I crawled over to the mirror and stared at my swollen form. I was turning into a monster; my face was no longer my own but was distorted by angry swollen blotches. I tried to find my mum but their bed was empty, they haven't come home. The food I cooked is untouched. I began to panic and I started crying furiously in pain. I was hit by the inspiration of calling a doctor and I ran to the phone, forgetting that my mother has hidden all of the batteries so I can't contact anyone. When I realized this I screamed twice as hard as if this had somehow doubled the pain. I doubled over. I knew I needed help, so painfully I pulled on shoes and a coat and stumbled outside, blinking frantically against the onslaught of snow hitting my eyes. I tried to run toward the doctor's surgery where I'd been once before but I could barely remember the direction it was in. After ten minutes I could hardly walk and I collapsed under a street lamp, my nightdress soaking through the instant it hit the snowy ground. I didn't even have the energy to cry. I just stared straight ahead, the pain all-consuming. I leant forward, the last pieces of logic I could cling to were screaming to keep moving and to get to the doctors surgery. I dragged myself along and made it to the large oak door. I collapsed on his doorstep as the world was painfully torn away from me.

The verdict was measles and then something else caused by the cold and exhaustion on top of that. The only good thing about it was that I got to watch my mother be yelled at by the doctor whom I took an instant liking to as I woke up to this. I was to be left in his care for a few days and was currently wrapped up in multiple blankets by an open fire. Even the pain seemed manageable now. He sat down beside me, taking my temperature and noting it.

"You're lucky we found you when we did." He shook his head. "You're lucky to be alive."

"What do you mean?" I asked croakily

"Well, any longer and I don't think you'd still be with us."

I stared at him questioningly.

"You probably would have died."

I gasped a little and tried to digest this. Sometime ago I had cried because I thought there was no escape, but now there was a second grief as I learnt the truth.

There is an escape. It could be painful. It could happen at any time. How utterly terrifying.

ANGELICA: 87 seconds

I scratch the date of that night onto my cupboard. It is the only time I have ever seen my Father angry and I etch it into the wood and my brain as a reminder that I never want to see him angry again.

School had been interesting and instead of annoying me as usual, Hannis fell asleep in class and, to my great amusement, snored. Mother had then, of course, made me cook the dinner while she danced around me, looking busy but not actually aiding the process at all. The question had occurred to me while I giggled at Hannis sleeping: what if I were a Jew? Would the teachers still like me? Would Hannis still want to pull my plait? Actually, I don't think there are any Jews left at our school. If I couldn't go to school, where would I be?

There is only one person I trust to give me the truthful answers to these questions.

"Dad," I take a deep breath and chew slowly on my boiled meat, "what is it exactly that the Jews did so wrong?"

Oddly my Mother looks like she is going to try and explain but she is cut off by the power that is Father angry. His plate crashes to the floor, and his chair too, as he leaps up and Tara starts to cry because of the noise (while ironically adding to it).

"Don't you ever say that again, do you understand?" His words are slow and loaded but deafeningly loud and each one stings like a blow.

I glare at him. "Dad," I try, but he looks stricken and begins to hit the table

"Angelica. Don't ever say those things to anyone. They will think you are a sympathizer. Do you want to be thought of as soft?" I glare at him in shock, terror and indignation and try desperately not to let any tears leak out of my loaded eyes. "Answer me!"

I push back my chair and run away from the table. I reach the front door and hesitate. I don't want to get caught in a bomb raid, but then I hear footsteps behind me and my anger is rekindled. I run, carrying what had just happened with me in my chest, like a ball of knotted wool and with the force of every exhale I try to untangle it from a different point, only to find that it gets tighter and my breath more shallow with hurt and frustration. Eventually all I can do is hug myself and cry. My prevailing thought is don't get too close to people because then you have to care about what they say, and people say horrible things.

SABINA: 1 minute

I had my suspicions the entire time that this was his plan. I begged to go back to Gran's, but apparently that made me selfish and ungrateful because millions of eleven year olds would love to have the opportunity to go to boarding school, particularly one as good as Castle. But I was not fooled by any of his persuasion. He said himself he can sell anything. The argument (which was the longest the three of us had spent in the same room as each other all summer) culminated in my yelling "Why take me away from Gran to ship me off to some boarding school?" which earned me a slap from my step-dad and a "Stop being hysterical" from my mother.

So here I am in a hospital-like bed, identical to the fourteen others around me. Our 'welcome talk' resembles a jail-guard's rule rather than a matron's and the lights are turned out instantly with the barked instruction that no one is to talk or leave their beds until

6.30 am sharp. I lie very still, becoming increasingly aware of how little I know about the other girls in the dorm. Everything is dead silent – is that normal? I can't remember sleeping in a room with another person and so every little creak instils a tightening in my chest and my palms grow damp with a panicky sweat. What if one of the others is psychotic? What if one of them is a werewolf and at midnight will begin to howl and prowl the room salivating, weaving between the beds until I feel jaws sinking through my flesh… hear the breaking bone. Or what if the whole school is possessed? That could be why they're so silent. Maybe this is actually a plot to kill me off and my step-dad's got them all programmed to attack at a certain time. I'm in the middle bed so I'll be trapped!

I pull the duvet over my head and lay very still, trying to muffle the sound of my breathing to make it more difficult for whatever horrors may be surrounding me to locate my exact position. But this seems like an extreme act of cowardice on my behalf which leaves a bitter pang in my stomach so, on the count of three, I quickly raise my head above the duvet and clench my fists ready to fight.

The rest of the first night passes in much the same way and it isn't until the early morning that the tension finally leaves my body and I am overcome by the only thing I have actually been battling against: sleep.

CLEMENCE: 1.7 minutes

I let the cigarette ash fall into the bubbles that surround our bodies and two of the girls laugh and ask for a smoke, which of course I provide. One thing I've learnt is that women like to get their own way; oblige them and often they'll be eating out of the palm of your hand. The second stage is a 'shy' compliment. My favorite choices are comments on their eyes, hair or smile; nothing too graphic yet, like tits, or else you scare them off. They're quite fragile creatures, easily charmed but equally easily offended. The third step is the sob story, which I change with each girl, altering it to fit the situation and her reaction. However, it normally consists of dead parents, being broke, bullied (they love that one – who'd have known my crappy childhood was good for something?) but then it is important to point out that I am now a self-employed business man and raking in the cash. This method has been carefully formulated, tried and tested by my good self and has had excellent results. When I look in the mirror now I no longer see the face of a loser. I see the things that the women I have been with have pointed out: tanned skin, strong features, young body and brooding eyes. Oh yeah, that reminds me; eye contact is bloody fantastic with women. Men think you're trying to stare them down or challenge them, but women see it as connection.

I always stop off in this spa on the way back from trading in Greece as it is filled with the bored wives of rich men who spend their days soaking in here to try and pass the time. I enjoy knowing exactly what to do now. I feel like the alpha male with lionesses fawning around him. At this very moment a women in a red two-piece swimsuit is running her hand up and down my thigh under the bubbles and another is dragging her fingers through my hair while I tell of a battle I barely made it out of in the war. Of course, they probably know I'm too young to have fought properly but it all adds to the excitement. They will let their minds create the image of 'the young brave soldier' and it is these romantic notions that keep them hooked. They laugh at my jokes as I watch the smoke escape their perfectly inked lips and we pass around a bottle of schnapps until everyone is thoroughly enjoying themselves. By the end of the evening I have five invites which I graciously accept, and I know that this is as good as it gets.

SABINA: 1.1 minutes

A whistle is being blown sharply into my ear. This is worse than waking up to my mother's notes, but I have no choice so I sit up obediently with all the other girls in my dorm. The whistle blower is a tall austere woman who looks like she was stretched as a child and never fully recovered. Her forehead has wrinkles but her eyes don't. This makes me instantly dislike her as to me that means she raises her eyebrows in disdain more then she laughs or smiles.

"My name is Miss Gesh and I am in charge of making sure you settle in," she says coldly. "Now, when I blow this whistle again you will have ten minutes to unpack your suitcases and fold your clothes neatly into you wardrobes."

The whistle sounds and everyone springs into fearful action.

"Four minutes left."

The pressure of a time limit starts to get to me as I look over at the girl next to me whose suitcase is nearly empty. I begin to throw a few things into the wardrobe to speed the process up. The whistle blows and the room freezes as Miss Gesh prowls by each cupboard inspecting it. My heart begging to race as she nears mine. I don't understand why she's doing this.

"Name?"

I look up nervously and my mind goes blank; it's my issue with being put under pressure again.

"Good God, child, have you forgotten your own name?"

There are nervous titters from the other girls which make my face burn and, thankfully, sense returns.

"Sabina Mangos," I say.

"Well, 'Sabina Mangos', you have clearly been spoilt. Look at the state of your cupboard. You are one of those children who has had everything done for them in the past."

I don't like her telling me who I am when she doesn't know me. And on top of that she is entirely wrong; at home I'm in charge of all the washing, folding and cooking. That's all I know! I laugh because she has got me so wrong but she doesn't look amused and with one easy sweep she sends all of my clothes, including the half that I so carefully folded, flying across the room where they litter the floor.

"Everyone else can go to breakfast. Sabina Mangos, you can clear up neatly this time."

I scowl as she leaves the room with the other girls. I feel humiliated, ostracized and misjudged and I feel the tears begin to roll down my cheeks in defeat.

"Hey, don't cry, I'll help you." The girl whose bed is on the left of mine is behind me. She's bigger than me, has short red hair and looks a bit like a picture of a pixie I saw in a Brothers Grimm story. We start to fold the clothes up together. "Don't worry about this," she says, gesturing to the whole predicament. "My sister went to this school and she told me about this and it happens to loads of people. You were just unlucky. That girl," she points to the bed opposite her, "had tons of sweets and chocolates with her and spent the whole ten minutes stowing them in the locked compartment. Look, she hasn't unpacked any of her clothes! She just got to you first, that's all."

"Thanks," I smile.

"I'm Molly, by the way." I nod. "And you, you are 'Sabina Mangos'." She does an uncanny impression of Miss Gesh's nasal voice and we both laugh as we head of to our first lesson.

Molly turns out to be a good person to have befriended as I would have never found the classroom without her.

But we are still late because of the unpacking thing. Luckily our English teacher, Mr. Franz, is jovial and welcomes us to sit at the last two desks which are right at the front of the class and have, mysteriously, been left free.

As the lesson begins I develop a theory that as we get older we forget how to feel. If you watch a baby, it savors every texture, smell, taste and sight. Adults either become bored with these 'trivialities' or so accustomed to them that they forget how to use their senses fully. Whatever it is, I conclude that Mr. Franz's sense of smell is no longer active as a second giant waft of garlic breath engulfs my face and I involuntarily wrinkle my nose and scrunch up my eyes against the onslaught.

***

Although I do love to focus on Sabina's memories, I now throw in a memory of a character from Angelica's life, because I feel the best stories are ones told from all sides. And, in all honesty, initially I did not think Hannis a man of substance or feeling and I like to be proved wrong. Sure enough, when his time came I ended up peppering the collection with some of his most prominent moments, not only to clarify and expand on the story but because I felt his life also deserved it.

HANNIS: 1.2 minutes

This year I dread the Christmas holidays. Without the distraction of school I know that stuff at home will be unbearable. It's not even the shouting I mind the most, it's when the silence hits and my mum's alone in her room, silently crying, and my dad in his armchair, silently smoking. Both seem to ignore my presence unless they're using me for ammunition against each other. I sit silently too and focus on Angelica's long black hair, a coy smile on her lips and a challenge in her eye, and this is what gets me through.

ANGELICA: 1.2 minutes

Father has decided that what the family needs is a break from work and war life. I know what has caused his change in attitude when he is normally so focused on work. He told Mother not to tell us but of course she pathetically blurted it out. Apparently the war effort is not going to plan and they are recruiting any men possible now, no matter what age. My father has been summoned and will leave next Tuesday. He, of course, looks on the bright side of this and forces us all to as well by saying we all may as well take the next few days off and go on our last family ski trip before he had to leave.

By Saturday morning we are out on the slopes in a warm white paradise and the snow seems to sparkle with promise. It is as if there is no war at all.

I always race my father and my mother skis slower with the little ones. However, I have a suspicion that he lets me win so today I search for real competition. The slopes are almost empty so I can't choose an unknown person. Then an idea occurs to me and I jet off close to the poles of the ski lift. I pick a chair that's being carried down the hill on the wire, memorize the yellow and red home front sticker on the back of it. I cut through the snow, frequently glancing up to locate my opponent: I'm catching up with it. I hear the unnerving crunch beneath my skis as ice replaces snow briefly and my pace accelerates, as does my pulse. I've sped up though and I'm determined to keep that speed. To slow down would be cowardly and might lose me the race. Lower down I hit a foresty patch and grit my teeth in annoyance. "Unfair differences in conditions," I mutter to myself, as I know the lift only has accommodating air to contend with while I have to dodge bushy ferns.

Finally I'm clear and glance up to check my opponent's position. He's ahead but the end of the lift is in sight and I snap my skis together, bend forward and shoot the last twenty meters. There is nothing but white noise and my ears feel like they will fall off but I am determined and I reach the queue line a good ten seconds before the chair I was racing trundles emptily round the wheel. I laugh exultantly. I love winning.

"Angie!" Dad yells, stopping beside me. "Good God, what a little racer you are!"

He pats me on the head and I grin at him. The air is so cold that we look like fire eaters as we talk, but something about it is intoxicatingly pure. I suppose that's how I always feel around my father: pure and focused and safe. Then my mother appears with Annabel and Tara, who is still snow plowing a way back, and stops nervously before the last drop, slowly examining the easiest route down, and the spell is broken. I am back to my usual self, feeling impatient and superior.

***

That evening her Father took her to the Christmas markets where they were staying and told her she could pick anything she wanted, regardless of price, and for the first time in her life she felt spoilt. The point of the trip had been to tell her of his law firm's work. I know this from sifting through his vague memories but he couldn't bring himself to do it. Eventually they came across a street artist and she decided she wanted her picture, as she was now, sketched. The artist was a man whom I would later find out spent too much of his life solemnly sharpening his tools while criticizing himself on his works' imperfections. A fact that was perhaps irrelevant as his paintings sold well and he never left the market in Garmisch. Angelica, however, was transfixed by the picture and stared at herself the whole way home, fascinated by the captured moment and by her own face.

SABINA: 1.2 minutes

"Are you Catholic?"

She was working her way through the dorm and already had two followers. I could tell that this would be the girl who held all the power. She was tall, curvy and well developed for her age and to look at her made me feel inferior.

"She's been asking everyone this all morning," Molly mutters under her breath to me, and as I turn around I'm looking up into those piercing green eyes.

"Are you Catholic?" Mona Stanzil drawls down at me. I think back to eating fish on Fridays at Gran's and to having to go to church every Sunday and how it was always an effort to try and stay awake. I didn't want to go to church again so I answered that I wasn't.

"My parents told me I'm only allowed to make friends with people who are Catholic," she informs me, as if I'd be interested, "so you're off the list."

She wheels past me so fast that I fall backwards onto my bed.

"You're such a little squirt," she laughs and I frown because I don't think that I suit that nickname at all. But for some reason it catches on and, by the end of the day, all the girls in my year except Molly are calling me it and I don't have the guts to tell them not to.

To add to my discomfort all of the meals are served cold and are disgusting. The worst has to be on a

Wednesday, which is always heart and rice, and not only the fact that it tastes like blood still and is brittle and chewy as it floats in your mouth, but it is also stone cold, reeks of death and the idea of eating the heart of something repulses me so violently that I gag every time I look down at my plate. But this place is unforgiving and anyone who doesn't eat it for Wednesday lunch is re-served it for supper, then breakfast the next day and lunch until you cave in to the hunger and eat it. They call it teaching us gratitude. It is now Friday so I haven't eaten for three days and I feel fatigued and like I'm shrinking. Sleeping on an empty stomach is hard but it's even worse when every night after lights out, I hear Rachel thud out of bed, unlock her treasure chest and munch her way loudly through chocolate bars while the rest of us lie there salivating in the darkness.

One night Molly asked if she would share and got a desk lamp thrown at her and a hissed "It's not my fault your parents don't love you as much as mine love me."

And so we all fall asleep to the sound of stomachs rumbling, rustled foil, snapping chocolate and chomping.

The second week I start piano lessons, which I begin to loathe, and I can feel my hatred of life increasing. My only solace is the time off we are given because I found an Enid Blyton novel while clearing up the library and I treasure it. Every time we have no lessons I run to the bottom of the grounds where I have found an old hollowed-out tree. I can curl up there undisturbed and shut out the world for hours reading about the adventures of the Famous Five. I want my childhood so desperately to be like theirs and so I relish these beautiful moments where I am part of their group.

Having just savored another delectable adventure, I race back up to the school so as not to be late for gym. When I reach the changing room I catch the tail end of an announcement that Mona's making to her followers about 'initiation' but they fall silent as I enter.

"Where's everyone else?" I ask.

"They're out already. We're late," she whispers conspiratorially and I smile back because I desperately want to be accepted into a group. Maybe I could even suggest calling us the Famous Five and ask Molly to join too, and a little spark of hope is kindled within my soul.

"Oh no," one of her followers states dramatically, "I left my games uniform in the gym cupboard."

Mona looks at me.

"I could get it for you?" I offer and they nod gratefully.

"Thanks squirt." I go into the cupboard and one of the girls yells, "It's at the back." as I crawl into the tight space at the back, I hear the door slam and my heart stops when I hear the lock click. I leap up and start banging on the door.

"Mona," I yell, "let me out."

I can hear the panic in my voice as I begin to thud my weight against the door desperately and hear the cackles from outside.

"All right calm down before you break something," she yells through the keyhole. "I'll let you out in ten seconds… if you keep quiet."

I step back from the door and calm my breath, counting down from ten in my head. Nothing.

"On second thoughts," her voice is strained as she fights against her oncoming giggle, "I think I'll take a walk instead."

"Mona!" I cry out desperately and I yell the worst abuses I can think of.

"Is that the best you can do, Squirt? See, this is why we chose you, cos you are don't know how to defend yourself," and with that parting blow I hear her leaving the room, dragging the key along the wall so I can hear that she has taken it with her.

I shut my eyes and think of the Famous Five and try to tackle this as if I am on one of their adventures with them. I start by searching for alternative escape routes. I finish this task in about thirty seconds as the room is very small. I then look to see if the hinges of the door can be removed somehow, but this again proves a short and fruitless task so I resort to banging and screaming and throwing myself against the door. I then get more inventive and start throwing things at it but nothing helps. I have a horrible notion that I am going to die in this cupboard, which fills me with such grief that I start to sob. What a pointless way to die. Of all the ways to go, what an unworthy death. It won't be noble or courageous; people will laugh at me.

"Oh yes, that girl who got locked in a cupboard and died, how stupid of her."

And eventually the gossip will get around to my mother and she'll agree.

Oh God. I can feel my head starting to spin. I look at my watch I've been here for five hours. She must have told someone by now, but I don't really believe that she would do that. It will be far more entertaining for her to see how long this can go on for. I puff out my cheeks and focus on some old song lyrics. I place my hands against either wall to stop the room from closing in on me and crushing me like in that Sherlock Holmes story.

Another half hour passes this way and then I feel cold all over with a new realization: I really need to pee. I start the panicking process all over again as desperation takes over rational thinking. I feel my throat contracting as I try and repress thoughts of how long I will be left in this pain.

Suddenly I hear voices.

"This way!" It's Molly's voice, love her! She must have raised the alarm when I didn't return to the dorm.

"Molly!" I shriek, "I'm here! Mona locked me in. Get me out!" By now I can hear several teachers. The pressure in my stomach increases and I wail desperately, "Get me out!"

"Stop getting hysterical." It's the voice of Miss Gesh and it makes me hit the wall with anger because if it was her, she'd be hysterical too. They are arguing about whether or not they can break the door down.

"A new door will be expensive," someone comments and I groan and dig my finger nails into my palms to try and distract myself from the fact that this is my pathetic life. It seems that Mona hasn't admitted to locking me in.

"Ask Mona!" I cry.

"Dear, we're going to call the fire brigade and they can pick the lock and get you out."

"No!" I wail and I begin to sob.

I know I will not be able to hold on that long. I double over and bite my fist, willing myself to keep it together, but then I succumb to the humiliation and I let the pain go. I take a deep breath and breathe a sigh as relief washes over me for a brief moment. Then I begin to cry uncontrollably as the pee cools on my clothes and I am crouched in a foul-smelling puddle, too drained and belittled to move.

Eventually a man in an orange uniform picks the lock and carries me out and I lay limply over his shoulder, defeated. Until I see Mona poke her head into the room and exclaim, "She's wet herself!"

I don't hesitate. I have never felt such all-consuming, white hot anger in my life and it pierces straight through humiliation and defeat. I throw myself at Mona and start pummeling her. I grab her hair and pull her over and scratch her until she starts to howl but I don't stop violently flailing until I am carried away and given fresh clothes.

LOUISE: 58 seconds

"Straighten your hat, Lou," Mother snaps at me from behind.

I hate that my name can be shortened to something that decent women can't even bring themselves to say, but it is fun to watch the shock on some of their faces when they test out my nickname themselves. I have only been persuaded out of the house because my mother has opera tickets for the family.

My day is defined by who I talk to. On days when I barely leave the house due to my studies, I become concerned about going out because any conversation I may have will then define the day. However, if it is a public day then so much speaking is done that I become confident with it and it doesn't matter if in some of the conversations I am uninteresting. I think about language a lot. English is my first language, but I also study French, Italian and German and it sometimes feels as if my life is dictated by words.

The thing that truly fascinates me is translation. For example, how can a word not exist in another language, and does that mean that its speakers lack that aspect of human nature? I don't think that can be possible but still some words simply can't be translated and so I use them in their organic form, rather than use a shadow of what I mean just so people can understand. As we walk to the opera, I use one of my favorites when a young gentlemen who has linked my arm exclaims, "I say, there's nothing quite like the view of the English seaside, is there?" and I reply by telling him that I think it is an "Augenweide." My mother quickly intervenes, "She's always doing this." She laughs heartily and tries to change the subject. Augenweide translates to something like "a meadow for the eye" and I don't think there's a better way to describe a beautiful sight.

Little did I know that tonight I would see the most beautiful sight I had ever seen.

ANGELICA: 1.4 minutes

I know it is bad news as soon as I hold the letter. It is too light to be one of Dad's carefully written stories that he sends home for us. I hide it up my sleeve as my mother approaches, wide-eyed, and pronounces her familiar morning greeting of "Any post?"

I don't know why I lie but this seems somehow personal and I hide behind the stairs before I look at it. I can't open it though. I'm terrified of the change it may bring to my life: of the despair. I hold the envelope up to the light and squint to try and glimpse what lies within. I see the word "alive" and rip into the envelope with all my will and focus on the fact that it won't bring bad news.

If there is a God, as my mother tells me, then now is the time to show himself.

'Mr Hammen has been taken prisoner by the Russian army. It should bring you some comfort that we have received confirmation that he is alive. We will update you should the situation change.'

I can feel the same cold tone with which the letter was written seeping into my veins and I hope it will freeze my heart over so I can die. But I don't, instead I begin to shred the letter with my teeth and nails as if it never existed. My mother comes around the corner, hearing the ruckus, and I throw the shreds at her and scream then run to my room.

Later that night I see her sobbing quietly in the kitchen. She has put them back in order, all of the tiny shreds of paper, even though she could have made sense of it without doing this. She knows what happens to prisoners of the enemy, and so do I.

* * *

I'm worried. I hate when you're enjoying a book and then authors suddenly take it to a serious level by putting one of the best characters in mortal peril. Sarah wraps her arms around me and kisses my cheek.

"You're looking very thoughtful," she chides.

I mark the page and turn the book onto its front, then pick up my much-needed coffee.

"Not really," I lie.

She grabs our breakfast plates and I push back my chair to start the washing up, while the girls get ready, even though I see Lisa sneaking out in to the garden in her pyjamas to say good morning to the animals first.

"I've got a dilemma," Sarah starts, and I am suddenly whisked back into the present, back to myself. The thoughts of all the others floating around my mind because I have read of them all night evaporate. "You know Albert from work?" she says, beginning to dry the plate I hand her. "Well, he fell asleep at the wheel."

"He's ok?" I ask.

"Yeah, yeah, fine, except he's lost his driving license and has asked me if I can register him for a British one and bring it out to him when I'm working in Germany next week. Is that possible?"

I frown. "It's asking quite a lot and I'm not sure it's entirely legal but you can probably do it."

"Yeah? Do you think I should?"

I laugh. "We both know you're going to do whatever you decide."

She laughs too. "I wouldn't normally, but he is the only person I can bear at my mum's company and he has helped me in dealing with her over the years. I feel like I owe him."

I look at her; she's such a stickler for repaying people for friendship and although I admire this, I also worry that she spreads herself to thin. Guilt and love rush through me; I see how hard she's been working and I hate myself for not being able to give her all that she deserves. I have no idea how she is so patient with me and I can't believe I've let my focus be so swayed from finding a job. I'm ridiculous, staying up all night reading, while my wife's been bringing home the bacon.

I impulsively and apologetically kiss her and resolve to have a job by the end of the day. Once she has left for work with the kids, I set out in earnest applying to anything I can get my hands on and making multiple phone calls. By 3pm I have exhausted both my mind and resources and, since all I can realistically do now is wait for a response, I justifiably open the book where I left off.

* * *

SABINA: 1.5 minutes

Since that incident I have been treated with slightly more respect and Mona has stopped her teasing – at least while her scars are healing. My main problem now is my teachers, especially Miss Gesh who is my German teacher. I have always liked German because I'm good at creative writing but everything I do in her lesson gets given an F, despite the fact that I think some of it is rather inspired. And other girls' pieces of work which are worse than mine get good grades.

Once a month we are allowed to be sent gift hampers from our parents. I get sent a small allowance and other girls are sent letters and clothes. Rachel's hamper is by far the most enviable though, overflowing with cakes that smell of cinnamon and butter icing, and bags of sweets, tins of biscuits and piles of chocolates. She quickly locks all this away in her cupboard and ties the key around her neck for safe keeping until lights out, when she feasts selfishly. We all lay awake, mouths salivating to the sound of every chomp as she shovels handfuls of the delicacies into her mouth and chews almost in slow motion to tantalize our grumbling stomachs. Something floats back into my mind when my stomach rumbles at night in-between her munches. It's Gran's voice talking of revenge, and on the brink of sleep one night I form a plan.

On an impulse, and because I've seen evidence of her commitment to "pranks", I recruit Mona who is willing to help. At midnight we creep barefoot down the cold stone floors to the kitchens. Once before a few of the girls went there to try and scavenge food but there was nothing appealing, just rice and cabbage. As we reach the door there is an overwhelming smell of cabbage and I have to cover my nose with my sleeve. Trying not to giggle, we roll several cabbages off the shelves and into an empty suitcase, then heave it with some difficulty back up to the dorm, which is silent. Knowing where the key is we unlock Rachel's cupboard and empty the contents into the middle of the room. When the cupboard is empty, we refill it with shredded cabbage, lock it and place the key back around her neck. I then quietly wake up the rest of the dorm by dull torchlight and we distribute every delicious piece of food between us and gleefully munch away while she snores. Mid mouthful, Mona catches my eye and says something. The words are distorted by the huge amount of cake she has in her mouth but I think what she says is, "You're all right Squirt" and for some reason it makes me feel safe.

LOUISE: 1.2 minutes

My mouth actually aches from trying to repress a smile and small bursts of laughter keep rippling out of me, which causes my mother to glare at me meaningfully. I am normally very composed but apparently not tonight. I think it was the eyes; they simply unraveled me. It was the way his eyes sang as much as the way he sang, with so much passion. As if anything were possible. All the eyes I look into on a daily basis seem afraid to be alive but not his. They were not modest nor tentative and seemed to override all social policies. They set you free, and to look in them fed your soul – fueled it with a passion and vitality which I'd never had. For two and a half hours I was strong, funny and beautiful, and all this caught me off guard. I would of course never have acted on this feeling which, once the music ended, had ceased to be within me for it hadn't come from me.

I went back to the opera on my own almost every night, hiding myself in the corner seat so I could just experience everything again; the fullness in my chest, the desire to leap up and clap my arms above my head.

Surprisingly it was my mother who took the next step for me at one of the frequent social gatherings at the main hall. Her way of conversing in social circles when I am with her is to present me to the groups of expectant eyes and effortlessly shift between bragging about me and chastising me. She is bringing up my skill with languages for the fourth or fifth time when I feel a hand on my arm.

"Well, that's most impressive girl. Are you fluent in German?"

I nod at the skinny, old, olive-skinned woman.

"Ah, you see we've been asked to tour with a German opera after our run here is finished and some of our more prominent players don't speak the language very well." She glances behind me and a warm smile fills her weathered cheeks out. "Isn't that right, Mr. Mangos?"

A booming laugh echoes next to me and I turn. He is round but it is not that that makes it seem as if he takes up the space. It's like there is too much life force surrounding him for people to enter the area around him, but I am being hit by the full brunt of it and I'm beaming. He has grabbed the old lady by the arm and the waist and is waltzing her round in a circle.

"Are you insulting me in front of pretty women again, Aldora?"

She cackles while the rest of the room looks on in mild horror at a display so obviously un-British but which I desperately want to be part of it.

Aldora pinches his cheek and croons, "I'll make it up to you by introducing you to the pretty woman, how about that?"

"Yes, yes I think that would be most proper." He turns to face me and attempts to imitate the stiffness of the other men in the room. He even tries a British accent.

"Madam." He bows dramatically, flourishing both arms, and kisses my hand. "If I profane with my unworthiest hand this holy shrine."

I know that he is making a joke of English behaviour, of all of us here, and of me, but I can't help but hoot with laughter. People I know in the room look on puzzled, clearly not seeing the *Romeo and Juliet* reference he used but I find it rather clever. He meets my eyes, seeing my understanding, and he boldly kisses both my cheeks which makes me blush furiously and him laugh and laugh at my reaction. I try to excuse myself to avoid this obvious display of emotion I've now become highly conscious of, but Aldora is explaining how I might teach him and a few of the others German. I had not actually agreed to this but I am too stuck to say anything. He turns to me, waiting for some kind of speech probably, but I am still in shock. He places a finger on my forehead, prodding my skin, and, I imagine, watching the red color return to the white the circle his finger left,

"Are you sure she's up too it?" he laughs. "It looks like it's going to take her a month to get over the shock of five minutes with us. Can the poor thing make it through an hour?" He nudges me casually and I still don't know how to react, torn between impulses. He laughs easily and pats my head, "If you're going to teach me, you're going to have to be able to handle me." And after another note of bewildered silence from me both of them are gone.

On the way home as I am replaying the evening's events in my mind and wincing at my parts. I begin to edit the way I acted, as if trying to rewrite the memory and the French expression *l'esprit de l'escalier* comes to mind. It means "the wit of the staircase", you know, when someone says something to you at the bottom of the staircase that you don't know how to react too and you only think of a good response once you've reached the top of the stairs and it is too late. I ponder over my perfect response to his parting blow implying that I couldn't handle him. I decide I should have told him that if he would have let me finish the Romeo speech and complete the action, then it would be him who could not handle me.

But that is an unladylike thought and, anyway, it is now too late.

***

Just to clarify that the next memories I collected from Angelica's story are many years after the last and so too, invariably, the one's from Hannis's. I suppose I can overview most of his university memories for you briefly to spare you some tedium, as initially they are fairly frivolous, at least in my opinion. Perhaps that's too harsh; maybe generic is a better description. Anyway, here is my sort of summary to update you on his situation in those years.

Friends came easily to Hannis, as did life. This could be attributed to any number of factors, however, his most obvious magnetic pull was his unaffected disposition, never stressed nor solemn and never taking life too seriously. It is due to this that within less than a month of joining the Boating Club at university, he was accepted to Rita's elite parties. Though her face was now frozen in a constant smile by the wrinkles that surrounded her eyes and lips, she held as much gravitas as her reputation suggested and the parties never failed to impress. Rita singled him out instantly; how could you not when he was suited up, hair slicked back and oozing boyish charm. He spent most of those parties by her side. She claimed he made her feel young again, and he would retort that beautiful women never age. It must have been more than seventeen years since a man paid her any real attention and I think she probably loved him for that.

He had a soft spot for women in general and on their first meeting had taken an instant liking to her. As the music and chatter swirled around them, and they leant against the edge of the wooden pier, and the evening sun made everyone unbearably beautiful to him, and his ecstasy of winning the boat race earlier that day made him feel important, she had asked what he was studying at university. He had talked of his business course.

"Yes, yes, just what I would have recommended," she had replied. "Charm is essential in business."

He had laughed and responded, "Why Rita, if you weren't over twice my age I would call you a flirt."

And with that they had sealed their friendship.

SABINA: 1.7 minutes

"Pay attention!" Miss Gesh snaps cracking the cane down on my left hand, as she always does in her class, and I gasp and straighten up, holding the tears back stubbornly. I have been leaning on my arm so long that there is an imprint of my ear on the skin. I actually was listening but I'm just sleepy because me and Mona were up whispering all night. We are assigned an essay and everyone begins to write furiously. I have a lot of ideas and grab the pen, then remember that I am not allowed to use my left hand and I switch it to my right. Miss Gesh says that writing with your left hand is a sin and each time I do, I am punished. Writing with my right hand is laborious and frustrating; it is like being five years old again, knowing what I want to say but being unable to forms the letters. Despite this, I get my ideas down, and though it is not perfectly coherent I'm confident that it has flair. I feel a sly sense of triumph that no matter how she tries to hold me back I will succeed.

When it is handed back to me with the usual red F, I am furious and Mona suggests that I copy out an actual poet's work for our poetry assignment to test if Miss Gesh is actually reading my work. Although I am scared, I do it. When this too is stamped with her mark, I find Mona to discuss payback. We brainstorm ideas and I come to the conclusion that grown-ups tend to swear if they really want to offend someone and most swearwords are directly linked with something smelly, for example "shit", "fuck", "bollocks". We deduce from this that the worst insult for a human being is to be linked with the onslaught of a foul smell. The plan is agreed upon: stink bombs.

On the day of the prank, my heart is beating hard. We knew which toilet Gesh always uses in the lunch break and it is outside the cafeteria. Just before German, which is the lesson before lunch, we both creep into this staff toilet and very carefully place one of the round stink bomb containers under the four points of the loo seat. We gently rest the seat back down, knowing that as soon as pressure is applied the foul-smelling liquid will be released. This is a show not to be missed.

As we are sitting down for lunch, a deafening shriek is heard by everyone in the canteen and the toilet door is flung open, letting both a flustered looking Miss Gesh and a foul smell escape. She runs down the edge of the canteen, opening all of the windows, yelling, "It was not me, that smell, that foul smell!"

By now the smell has reached everyone who is trying to eat their lunch and it really is vile. Cutlery is dropping back to the table faster than flies from an old lamp and slowly the giggles began as with each flustered protest she condemns herself as the culprit more and more. Mona and I are beside ourselves with triumphant hysterics. The teachers' table is divided between appalled looks and outright laughter until the principal escorts her from the room to a round of applause and me and Mona high-five under the table.

***

I have been strict in resisting commenting or taking over the telling of the stories like a jealous artist who wants to take credit for them. But now I feel the need to bridge the time gap as Angelica's next memory occurs several years after the last. We now find Angelica as a diligent university student, bright, young and ambitious, and attracting a fair amount of attention. She has chosen to study law, just as her father always hoped, and her favorite pastime is to snub the advances of hopeful boys. That is not to say that she does not encourage their advances; she was fully aware of the power she holds and indeed, wakes early every morning to fix herself just right. She retouches her hair and makeup each break time so that the image she projects never faded.

One morning she is hurrying through the corridor when a familiar voice stops her.

"I love the way your shoes sound in the empty hallways."

She rolls her eyes. "What do you want Hannis?"

He seems to think that the fact he's known her for years makes him different from all the other boys.

"Easy." Chastised, he holds up his hands in a position of surrender. "I just wanted to know why you never hang out with me any more?"

Although she finds his advances annoying, her friends always hang around her when Hannis talks to her and laugh too loudly while standing at odd angles, which they feel show themselves off best.

He laughs again and continues. "Actually I came over to ask you a favour. One of my friends needs a map reader, someone who's good with detail and is smart and I recommended you." She glances to the table outside where his mates are drinking beers, despite it only being 11am.

She raises an eyebrow. "Is this for one of your cronies?"

Hannis runs with a very popular crowd of men who all take part in some kind of sport, get a lot of attention from girls and tend to think that they are funnier and more important than they actually are.

"Yeah, a buddy of mine, he's a rally car driver. It's a compliment really, he's been real fussy on who to choose and I know you'd need to get it right, which makes you reliable." She begins to walk away. "Besides it'll look good on your CV the fact that you took a job already, the fact that you do something besides just study."

She glowers, "I'll think it over."

ANGELICA: 1.7 minutes

I swing the helmet in my hand and follow the directions the man at the gate gave me. I see one of the guys Hannis is always hanging out with leaning against a white car and marking a route on a map. He looks up casually and his eyes narrow as he sees me. Not the greeting I was expecting.

"Problem?" I ask curtly.

"You're a girl," he throws back equally coldly.

I stare at him for a moment. "Evidently not what you were expecting."

He sighs. "Evidently... I'm Jack."

"Angelica." I hold out my hand and he shakes it briefly.

"Oh, as in the Angelica," he laughs as he gets into the driver's seat. "Get in then, thought you were supposed to be efficient," he continues, though his voice is muffled as he puts on the helmet.

He starts the car before I've shut the door and I yank my seatbelt and helmet on angrily.

"What do you mean by 'the Angelica'?"

"Was that supposed to be an impression of my voice?" he asks in a convincing imitation of mine, which throws me and I laugh. I glance down at the map, ready to focus on the task at hand. "Take a sharp left in two hundred meters."

He complies.

"I just meant that your Hannis's girl."

I freeze. "I'm not Hannis's anything," I snap. "I hate the way you guys always say that, 'your girl', 'his girl'. I'd never say 'my boy."

"So he's not your boy?"

"No!... Turn right."

"Well, he seems to think he is," Jack continues, "he always talks about you." I roll my eyes. "Says you even kissed him back when you were kids."

I snort with laughter. "He used to try and hold my hand on the way back from school and that is about the extent of our relationship."

Jack suddenly hoots with laughter. "That's classic. Man, poor guy, he has this whole fictitious romance going on."

I've stopped reading the map temporarily, too annoyed by this revelation to concentrate, and I suddenly come back to my senses.

"Right!" I yell and Jack reacts instantly, spinning us round so fast that I drop the map but he's howling with laughter.

"I hate adrenaline junkies," I mutter, as I try to find the page we were on.

"I must say, he's got you totally wrong."

"In what way?"

"Well, you're mean."

I'm not sure if this statement wounds me or makes me proud.

"Unlike some people," I shoot a glare at him, "I've had to learn to be tough."

"Are you Bavarian?" he asks, speeding up. Adrenaline is slowly seeping through my veins and I'm fighting back a laugh. "Some of my relatives yeah. Why? Do I look Bavarian or something?"

"Nah, I just remembered this old Bavarian saying my mum once told me and I have a sneaky suspicion that it will suit you right down to the ground." He looks at me to check I'm listening,

"Eyes on the road!" I yell, hitting his helmet.

There is a pause. "Oh for God's sake... what's the saying?" He pauses again, dramatically, and for some reason I really want to know what he has to say. "The saying goes that those with Bavarian blood are wonderful to be around if you're nice to them, but if you cross them you're in trouble." I ponder this for a moment and I quite like it. "Hmm," he continues, "actually maybe that's not a very good fit because I haven't done anything wrong by you and yet you still haven't been exactly charming company."

"Actually, you pissed me off at the start."

"How?"

"You were narky about me being a girl."

"You think I want to be given directions by a woman?"

"You think I want to be driven by an asshole?"

He nods his head slowly. "Touché."

***

And that is how Angelica met Jack and started a chain of events that would bring heartache and neglect to many involved. But for now they are just young and ignorant of the rare occurrence they have just experienced where two genuine soul mates have the luck to meet. I enjoy looking at these early days more than some of the things to come, as when I look at them, perfectly preserved, I can almost fool myself that the rest never happened. One of the most infuriating parts on this job is that people barely ever realize or are conscious of when they are happy. I want to intervene to yell out, "This is a good moment for you, one of your best," but it is past and by the time they relive it, it is too late for the realization.

ANGELICA: 2 minutes

That evening I return home feeling more buoyant than I have since my father returned home from the war. I can still remember my excitement for the reunion. My mother had had to fight so hard to make all the arrangements and it had still been a year and a bit after the war ended before he was brought home. But the instant I saw him, I knew something wasn't right. He was a ghost of a man, no longer impressive or authoritative but weak, damaged.

My mother of course continues as if nothing is wrong, kisses him, cooks him breakfast, but I have never been one for the charade and I cannot hide my disappointment and hurt. He never talks of the Russian war camp; he barely talks at all. Only for business matters. He's just about managed to keep his law firm going and I help out, not out of love anymore, but out of a sense of duty to the man I did love.

***

Sabina's return home for Christmas was anticlimactic, to say the least, for despite herself she enjoyed boarding school, partly because she could resent it. She did not, however, wish to resent her family and had promised herself that she would make an effort not to argue with her mum or her step-dad and to try and visit her Gran. The latter part of this plan was instantly shattered by her mother's announcement of a ski trip-a, ploy, as I know from searching her memories, so that Sabina could not run back off to her Grandmother's.

SABINA: 2 minutes

The morning is always excellent. The sun on the snow and my face gives me so much love for everything around me that I start to tear up and I race down the slopes, embracing the speed and screaming at the top of my lungs, which my mother tells me not to do every time we have to get on a lift. However, after lunch fatigue always sets in and I want nothing more than to go back to the room and curl up with a good book. Neither of the grown-ups seem to grasp this and they push me to my limit till my thighs are burning and my cheeks have been slapped by cold and the tears from the morning are back, but this time they are unpleasant. The problem is that I have to catch up with them in order to ask to stop. I yell out to them and I know that they can hear me but they always keep me just in view but keep skiing.

At the bottom of the mountain, in the queue for a chairlift, I beg to stop for a hot chocolate. My step-dad grunts and rolls his eyes aggressively, saying, "I want to die!" (Which I think is a little melodramatic.) My mum simply refuses.

"We only just bloody stopped for lunch and we have to wait for you to catch up on every run anyway."

I begin to cry, hurt that he is rubbing my own incompetence in my face. My mum, not wanting the fuss, swears then adds, "I come on holiday to relax, so if going to a café will shut her up, let's go."

He grumbles and swigs from his hipflask, shrugging, "You should tell that kid to be more fucking grateful."

In the café there is an open fire and I order a hot chocolate (I have one every day and it is always the highlight) then I take out the book I'm reading, unbuckle my ski boots and begin where I left off. I look up when I feel my mum staring at me.

"You're such an unsociable child, Sabina, why do you read all the time?"

"I find it fun."

My mother looks totally taken aback and I know that she can't comprehend the concept of reading for enjoyment. She had said to me yesterday that I already knew how to read so reading more wasn't giving me another skill and there was nothing to actually achieve by reading. Normally she would ask, "How many books have you read since last time?" This translated into a measurement she could understand for when she read, it was to see how fast she could finish her book compared to you. I like to savor each line and sometimes re-read paragraphs again to try and rinse every last bit of detail and meaning from the words. My mother would often comment on the amount of books I've read with exclamations such as, "Not as many as last time."

And so my characters and their secrets remain hidden, just like my own from my mother, through nothing more than incompatibility. Yes, I know that sounds harsh but I have always thought of us as incompatible. I excuse myself and go to the loo to escape the rest of the conversation and when I get back my hot chocolate has arrived. I wrap my hands around it, lovingly anticipating the soothing warmth that will soon fill me up, and I start my ritual of carefully stirring the cream in until I am satisfied that it is ready to drink and I take an eager sip. I feel my brow furrow slightly in confusion as my brain tries to make sense of why it does not taste as expected. I stir it a little more and decide that I just didn't have enough, so I take a gulp. Instantly my mouth is filled with a white hot searing pain that hits the back of my throat, like when sea water gets up your nose and the taste is horribly bitter and sickly fruity fused with chocolate and lumps of cream. I wince and stare up in shock to see my step-dad staring at my facial expression and rocking with laughter while knocking back the schnapps in his hipflask which he wiggles at me and winks. I scoot back my chair and run outside to shovel the cold, pure snow into my mouth, scratching it across my tongue to try and get rid of the vile taste. I hate him. I know he spiked my hot chocolate with Schnapps, the vulgar old drunk! I feel sick and hurt, but I'm most upset about the hot chocolate. I know that's ruined for me now. He's taken away that pleasure. The mere idea of the smell of what was once my favorite drink now turns my stomach.

CLEMENCE: 2.3 minutes

I leave the two women asleep and sprawled on the bed and glance at the clock: 4.33am. I wander clumsily around the room, collecting my uniform and finishing off any of the alcohol we left. I don't sleep well most of the time; my mum would have said that's due to a guilty conscious, but if I was prone to that sort of thing then I wouldn't have stolen the blonde one's packet of cigarettes before I sneak out.

I amble through the town in the fresh night air and allow myself to be relaxed by the smoke as I exhale. My head clears a little from the alcohol and weed I use to fog it up and I can ponder the future. I like making plans and I like change, but there is also an argument for the 'if it ain't broke don't fix it' approach. I enjoy being a waiter at the Hotel der Samten, women sticking wads of cash and room numbers into my pocket as I take their luggage or orders. My life feels full. I feel satisfied. Who am I kidding? I get to live out a fantasy as a suave womanizer and most of the time that is enough. That is what I am. It is in the early hours of the morning, alone and reflective, that I feel the darkness seeping back into me, a resentment from childhood. With that thought I stub out my cigarette and take the cash (a mixture of wages and "tips") out of my pockets and count up what I've accumulated. It's a fair sum.

Halfway through counting, I feel a presence behind me. I leap around, wrapping my hands around the thief's throat and smash his head against a wall. I can hear myself yelling "Don't give me a reason to kill you because I will, and I'll enjoy it, I'm in that kinda mood."

It's only then I recognize the terrified bug eyes as Henry's, the annoying receptionist at the hotel. He looks shaken and I quickly brush him off and assume my persona.

"Ha ha, scared you there, didn't I? You should've seen your face."

He is rubbing his neck slowly and a nervous laugh escapes him, "Jesus Christ... you can't half be scary sometimes, Clemence."

I give him an easy smile. "How many times have I asked you not to call me Jesus Christ?"

He laughs a little but is backing away. "I just came out to ask you for a smoke but I should get back now." He turns and scuttles away.

"Henry!" I boom after him and I enjoy watching him squirm to a halt and turn like a man caught at gun point. I hold him there for a few extra seconds. "Best not sneak up on people when they're counting money, right?" He nods and is gone.

I duck into a nearby bar, feeling that the encounter is a sign that I should start afresh and leave my life at the hotel behind. But it's also made me feel confrontational.

"Drink?" the bristly barman asks.

I scan the shelves behind him, they all look dusty.

"What's your best drink?" I ask. He shrugs. "How can you not know what your best drink is? It looks like you've worked here long enough." He bristles more but I smile it off. "Go on, I know it's probably been a while... but try... try with all your might... to connect what I just said to you with an answer that you have to come up with yourself. It's quite simple really; we call it a conversation."

I maintain eye contact, smirking at his reaction as he scowls, crossing his arms.

"I'll kick you out of the bar," he grunts.

I leap up instantly. "Excellent idea, be rude and aggressive to your only customer. Wow sir, you really do have a stunning intellect. You have just refused service to probably the only profit you'd make for today."

He is now shuffling from foot to foot awkwardly, so I lean in closely. "I'll take the bottle at the back... half price."

I sit in the far corner, hugging the cool bottle, and enjoy the lick of alcohol as it stokes my soul into a pleasant abyss.

***

The thing that always strikes me when I study humans is that, unlike animals, they have the capability to suffer twenty-four hours a day because of thoughts. In my opinion Clemence suffered greatly at his own hands and I recall that at this point in my retrieval, I was struck by the idea that if someone just guided him the way a little, perhaps he could have been fixed.

ANGELICA 2.3 minutes

It becomes a summer of love and rally racing. After that first day, I was hired and I'd meet Jack for training three times a week, as well as being his partner during tournaments. He's the only person who makes me laugh. Once I saw a comedy show and the thought occurred to me that the rest of us are cursed because we cannot laugh alone. But with him, the curse is lifted. On days when I see him, I don't wake up early to do my hair and fix my face. I just go, and when I pull the helmet off after racing and my hair's sticking up all over the place and sweat is trickling off my forehead, I don't get annoyed and infuriated that I don't have a brush on me. Jack will just push my hair out my face, both of us high on the excitement of a race.

The first race we won was brilliant. As a semi-professional rally driver as young as he is, he's beginning to get noticed and some of the races even get televised. The day we won happened to be one of the aired ones, and as we mounted the podium there was a buzz of cameras and reporters who swarmed him like starved mosquitoes. His dad handed him this huge bottle of champagne and shook it laughing, telling him to aim well and he aimed straight for me, hidden slightly in the crowd. He got a bunch of the reporters too, pissing everyone off, and before I had time to dry my face or be annoyed, he pulled me to the front of the crowd and whispered "Not without you" in my ear. And then we kissed for the first time, our lips tasting of champagne that seemed to fuse with my blood, making me sweet and bubbly and ignorant of the crowds and hopelessly intoxicated.

He had refused the rest of the interviews lined up, which he should have done from a publicity point of view, and took me out to a pub at the seaside instead for a celebratory drink. I knew this pissed his father off but he didn't seem to care when I mentioned that.

"Well, now he'll hate me."

"He can't hate you. I've started winning since you came on the scene. As far as he's concerned you're a good luck charm... and what does a good luck charm drink?"

"I'll have a gin and tonic."

He scrunches his face up, "Predictably classy."

I laugh as he swaggers away to order at the bar. I hear roars of laughter from the corner of the room and see a table compiled of all Jack's raucous mates and Hannis too. I guess they must have been at the race. Hannis raises his glass in and my direction and I smile and hope he won't come over but, of course, he does. The chair scrapes back and he approaches with the confidence of beer and kisses me on both cheeks over-enthusiastically.

"Fantastic race. I knew you and Jack would make a good team."

"You have a talent for head hunting," I reply.

"You know what, though..." He pauses and offers me a swig of beer. "I thought us three would all hang out more. You know, we've been friends for a long time and Jack funded my sailing training. I'm the link between you two."

"Mmmm hmmm." I begin to tap my fingers on the table.

"Nice publicity stunt by the way... your idea or his?"

"What?" I caution, raising an eyebrow.

"The kiss."

I lean in so that I am inches away from his jealous little face and whisper, "Impulsive actually."

He eyes me carefully then glances at the bar behind me. "You don't really think he meant it? I mean look at him." He points behind me and I see a group of excitable girls surrounding him, a leggy blonde writing her number on a napkin for him.

I turn back to Hannis, "Do yourself a favor and go back to your table Hannis."

"Do you want to go out with me?"

"No," I say calmly. "Now go back to your table."

He reaches for my hand and I pull it away.

"Angie," he chides in a soft cooing voice reserved in my book for dogs and babies, not potential love interests.

At that moment Jack strides back over. "God, we don't half look ridiculous," he grins, gesturing to the all-in-one white racing suits we haven't changed out of yet. "Although," he tilts his head studying me, "somehow you still manage to pull it off."

I feel colour rising to my cheeks because of how intensely he looks me up and down and there's a strange fullness in the pit of my stomach. Jack continues talking and flips the napkin he's holding to Hannis.

"More your type of thing than mine I think," he says flippantly, then shrugs, taking a sip of his beer. "I like brunettes."

Hannis folds the napkin up slowly, then deliberately wishes us both a good evening, pats Jack on the back and leaves the bar. I gulp down the gin and tonic.

"That was awkward"

Jack laughs easily, "Why?"

"I think you're making him crazily jealous," I say honestly and Jack ponders this, looking serious, then meets my gaze and says gravely, "I can see why." He leans back. "I mean I'm smart, funny, have an excellent jawline and I'm well on my way to becoming an acclaimed rally car driver."

I grin. "I suppose that is enviable and your jawline's ok," I say, running my thumb across it and I catch the group of giggling girls staring jealously at me. "Those girls can't keep their eyes of you," I tease,

"Look who's jealous now?" he laughs and tickles me till I laugh too. "But you know what? You're right, everyone in here is bringing the mood down. Let's... you want to get out of here?"

I drain my drink to show I'm ready and he does the same. "Oh, look at that, both are drinks are gone, ah, time to go."

The evening air is warm we run out on to the beach behind the pub and crash down into the sand when neither of us see that there is a sudden drop. This makes me cackle with laughter and he shoves me away.

"You think you're so perfect but you fall like everyone else," I howl.

"Hilarious!" he scowls. "Stop laughing!" he pauses. "Angelica, are you a light weight by any chance?" he smirks suddenly,

"It's not the alcohol, it's you," I blurt out and I stop laughing. "You make me feel good." He smiles. "Don't get cocky, though. I've also had champagne and gin and tonic and I never normally drink."

"Still, a rare compliment," he shrugs. "I shall treasure it... may be years before another one comes along."

The sun is hitting his face beautifully and his eyes are glistening like portals into a better place and as I stare at them, I believe that this boy has all the answers to my happiness. I tune back into what he's saying. "Waiting for a compliment from you is like a drowning man waiting for rescue; if a float comes along he grabs a hold of it for dear life!"

I frown. "Are you trying to seduce me?"

Now it's his turn to howl. "By talking about life rafts?" He rolls onto his side, facing me and trying to suppress the laughter. "Yep, yep, that's my line, I talk about drowning men." He looks at me, calming down. "You underestimate me. If I was going to seduce you I'd say that although I find you very attractive in this suit... I'd prefer to take it off you."

There is a loaded pause as we look at each other.

"Why don't you then?" I challenge.

Testing whether I'm calling his bluff, slowly he rests his hand on the zip that runs along the side of the suit, keeping eye contact with me. I shrug and he slowly pulls it down, his hand trembling very slightly. I feel the warmth of the sun now caressing my exposed skin. I wriggle out of the suit so I am in just my underwear and smirk at his surprised expression.-

"Would you rather I put it back on?"

He smiles easily, "No, that's ok."

He very gently touches my face, watching for my reaction, and when I smile in acceptance he suddenly kisses me hungrily, like he's being dying to do that since the day we met. I kiss him back filled with so much passion, longing and happiness that it aches and overwhelms me. My fingers slide his zip down too and rip the suit off him and travel over him until we both begin to laugh. I lean my head against his chest to feel how his laughter and breathing sound so close to my own, because at that moment it is very special and touching to me that this person, this human being, is capable of laughing and breathing.

"Our lips are covered in sand," I say looking up at his face and brushing the sand off.

"Yeah," he grins, "we're both rather more enthusiastic then expected."

He touches my lips, then groans and shakes his head.

"Not yet... ok, I need to cool off." He slides me off him gently, then stands and pulls the rest of his suit off so he is just in his boxers. "You coming?"

"No," I say sprawling out and enjoying the last of the sunshine.

"Come on... you do that to me and then you don't even have the courtesy to join me in a swim?"

"Well, it's just not really the done thing... to go swimming in our underwear rather than proper bathing suits. I'll get in trouble if someone sees us."

He gestures at me in disbelief. "You weren't worried about driving me crazy five seconds ago!"

"Yeah well, we're hidden here."

He suddenly scoops me up over his shoulder and I scream and laugh.

"Who gives a shit about what people think."

He's halfway to the water's edge now.

"Wait, no my hair, my hair can't get wet," I shriek.

He stops briefly with mock concern. "Oh God, wait. Yeah, you're right, I didn't think about the effect this may have on your hair." And then he throws me in and laughs as I surface with dripping wet hair covering my face. I splash him and he runs.

That was the first night that Jack became one of my dream people. That night when the ice turned around I had to choose between Jack and one of my friends. I chose Jack to live. The shock of this probably was what woke me up, but it might also have been some kind of foreboding feeling as when I opened my eyes a light was shining directly into them.

I scrunch my eyes and realize that the light is coming from the bathroom down the hall. The door has swung open slightly. I climb out of bed, hissing my sisters' names, ready to give them what for waking me up the night before an exam, but when they don't answer I feel my heart sink.

I think I know what I'll find before I push the door. The wood is cold and the room reeks of shit. My father is naked and slumped on the toilet seat and I know he is dead because my mother is in the corner, just staring at him and shaking uncontrollably. I want to cover my nose and my eyes from the onslaught, but I can't move. I begin to cry. I would've rather he'd died at the war camp, far away, that we were told it was noble, because right now there is no mistake there is nothing more degrading then this. I begin to howl like a feral animal being electrocuted and the sound doesn't stop. Now when I think of my father, that's all I can hear.

* * *

It's early Saturday morning and I'm the only one awake. I feel a bit shaken by what I have just read and place the book under the bed as if this will erase the visceral image I now have in my mind. I think back to my own father's death and then shut my mind down; it's a place I won't get back from easily. I decide to combat this by focusing on the now and tiptoe into Lisa's room, waking her up with the promise of teaching her how to milk the cows and she readily agrees. It was always mine and Sarah's dream to be able to support our family ourselves by living on a farm. It's where we first met and when I don't mind the early starts, it is wonderful to have fresh milk and eggs every morning and good quality food.

Once Lisa seems to have gotten the hang of it, after a couple of false starts, she demands a story as we work. I have never been much of a story teller. I can barely even lie, I start to sweat and smile ridiculously. But she is waiting expectantly with full faith that I will have something brilliant in store. And so I turn to the first thing that crosses my mind and tell her of little Sabina's piano lesson. Being of a similar age, she laps it up, hooting with laughter, and as we carry the milk back she sighs, saying that that one is one of her favorite stories. I look at her, thinking for a moment she means she has heard it before but then realizing she must mean that it has been added to her collection.

Family time is precious and was undervalued in both mine and my wife's lives when we were children, so we make a point of trying to treasure it as best we can with all the demands that work brings. Neither of us mention that she will have to leave again on Sunday evening. It's a hard toll on an otherwise happy family. The girls always seem to cry and beg to go too, like they used to before they had to go to school. We spend a blissful day at the beach, all snuggling into a spot chosen by Phoebe among the sand dunes. We feast on luxurious cous cous salad that my wife has perfected and share fresh avocados. The afternoon is spent hosting boogie boarding competitions among ourselves which Lisa seems to have quite a knack for.

Late Sunday evening, after we have tucked the girls in with the promise that Mum will bring home the fresh Brezens from Germany that they love, I have to kiss my wife goodbye again. I sit in my empty room and suddenly feel quite alone. I hurriedly search for the book, knowing this will bring me a little more peace and I am satisfied when I find that I left it on Sabina's story. As I read, it makes me feel closer to my wife.

* * *

SABINA: 2.2 minutes

I sit on my bed cross-legged, pretending to polish my shoes as we're instructed to do every night. Mona is sprawled at the other end, clutching my pillow and talking animatedly. I'm not quite sure how we became best friends. I've been thinking about it, and even though I like Molly better as a person, Mona is definitely my favourite, which is strange. She suddenly leaps up and kisses the Marc Bolan poster that we stuck up between our beds. We both agree that he is gorgeous and frequently annoy the other girls by playing 'Get It On' loudly while jumping from bed to bed.

"God, I wish I was that tiger!" she exclaims (the picture is of him straddling a tiger) and I roll my eyes because I don't know what to say.

We've been discussing families. I told her about my Christmas and, to make me feel better, she launched into a dramatic recital of her parents' marital problems. She knows her mum cheats on her dad but her dad has no idea, and what's worse is that her mum uses Mona as a confidant for all the intimate details of extramarital escapades.

"Don't you mind that?" I ask, curious.

"Not really, not any more. It just really makes me want a boyfriend."

Again I'm quiet; Mona is all too easy to provoke into mood swings.

"Oohh, can I borrow this top?" she asks, pulling something out of my cupboard.

"It'll probably be too small on you," I say, looking at the red shirt which hangs from her fingers.

Her eyes narrow. "Well Squirt, it only hangs off you because you have absolutely no boobs at all and you're probably scared it will look better on someone with an actual figure," and with that she storms off to the toilets to try it on in private probably, in case it doesn't fit.

I decide to hang out with Molly for a while instead and agree to go round to her house at the weekend.

Molly lives just down the road from our school and no one knows why she bothers boarding. Just before we knock on the impressive doors to her grand house, Molly hesitates and says, "I don't usually bring people home… My mum… she's special… I trust you to understand."

I nod, now worried that this is going to turn into some kind of horror story but the door opens to reveal the most glamorous woman I have seen in real life. Her hair is expertly curled and then piled up impossibly round her face and her makeup is exquisite to the point that her features look otherworldly. The kind of dress only a woman can wear floats around her body. I am simultaneously in awe and jealous that Molly's mum is so wonderful.

She beams down at us absently and hurries us inside. Patting Molly's head she trills that we will have to play up stairs as she is very busy. She spins around the room, adjusting a tea set laid out on the table and muttering that everything has to be perfect. I'm intrigued, and before Molly can drag me up the stairs, I inquire as to who she is expecting. She turns, elegantly, to face me and says "Vivien Leigh". I'm in shock. I can't believe I am going to meet a movie icon. I have no idea what I'm going to say. Maybe Molly's mum could get me a part in one of her films. I'm looking down at my faded jeans and wishing I had borrowed one of Mona's dresses.

"I didn't know your mum was a movie star, Mol!" I accuse her.

Molly sighs, "She's not."

"She looks like a movie star."

"She wanted to be when she was younger, I think."

"Why have you never talked about her at school? She must have had such an interesting life! God, this is exciting!"

"Bini, can I explain something to you..." she begins, but she is interrupted by her mother's honeyed voice. "Girls, why don't you join us for tea."

I leap up and check myself in her mirror then take the stairs two at a time.

Molly grabs my arm looking worried. "Promise me you'll act normal."

I'm insulted; is she saying I'll embarrass her?

"Of course,"' I reply curtly.

We enter the room and her mother pours two extra teas.

"Vivien, you know my daughter and this is her friend." She gestures in my direction and I look around the room but there is no one there. "Help yourself to tea and cake, girls, we certainly have been," she giggles conspiratorially with the chair opposite her and I stare in amazement. "We have other guests arriving later, but we wanted to catch up with you before the party starts, didn't we?" There is no one to answer her but she stares at the chair intently then smiles. "Well, that's true… and he couldn't keep his eyes off you!" She winks at us. "I expect you two know what we're talking about by now."

I nod, smiling awkwardly, unsure as to what is happening.

"Molly, why don't you update Viv on what's happened since last time."

Molly stares at the chair and flushes deep red then slowly and coldly recites stories from school about teachers and homework. Her mum nods and adds to parts of the recital, then turns her full attention back to the chair.

"She's going through a sulky stage at the moment I think, but she'll grow out of it…"

She continues to chat freely to no one, pausing and reacting in a manner so convincing that it is almost like a scene from a well-rehearsed play. But this is real and I spend my evening agape, watching a display of human behavior so profound and sad that I can barely hold back tears. Molly's mum is clinically insane for sure, but also, I realize, so sincerely disappointed in her own life with so much longing for how it might have been that living in a fantasy is vital to her survival. Instead of a funny charade the whole thing is deeply moving and horribly scaring.

After a while Molly excuses us by pretending we are in a school play which we must get back for and I thank her and Vivien before leaving. As soon as we're outside, Molly starts to cry and I just hug her, hardly believing what I've just witnessed. I know we won't talk about it again and that I won't tell anyone but I guess she just needed someone to know; someone in real life because I sense that Mol is not part of the fantasy life. Her mother has sort of mentally erased her and yet she has to humor her because it is illness, not cruelty. I know that tonight is one of the saddest things I've seen.

MANGOS: 4.2 minutes

I had been thoroughly annoyed that we were performing a German opera; I had grown to love Italian and I chose to speak in it amongst some of my closer companions in the company. It made me feel educated and charming and I liked the fact that it was lyrical even, without a musical score assisting it, but this actually hid its directness. The language forces you to be direct and I appreciate this. Only the main performers have to attend the German lessons. The chorus simply learn the words required but we must aim to perfect accents. In my opinion German is not musical; the words aren't so compatible with music. They protest against it with the fierceness of a virgin stopping unwanted advances.

After meeting the teacher, though, I am hopeful. Yes, she is English and brought up in that 'God forbid they feel an emotion' way! Squash it down, repress it! An attitude that makes me laugh and is the subject of many jokes among my companions, but I feel her soul has potential and I wake up with a smile on my face. The room is small and she leaps up as we pile in and basically blushes then busies herself with shuffling papers as we eventually take seats and look at her expectantly.

"I've been hired to teach you German basics," she begins, catching my eye briefly. "What is your preferences in terms of the language these classes should be taught in, as I know most of you are Greek but you sing in Italian and I assume you know some English?"

"You speak Greek?" one of the boys chimes in.

"No, but my Italian is fairly good."

I want to see this pale English rose speak in Italian for entertainment purposes so that is what is decide upon. This is perhaps a mistake as the picture and the sound are so odd it's like an old film that has been dubbed by a different actor to the original and all of us are struggling not to laugh. Eventually she begins to get flustered and looks on the verge of tears, so I take pity on her.

"We like your teaching," I assure her, "it's just that you are so un-Italian that it's... well... funny."

"Well, you're all so Greek that it'll be a miracle if we get anything done."

There is a pause where she looks scared at what has just escaped her lips and I think I can see her leg shaking.

"Ah," I state, "that is much more convincing Italian attitude."

She laughs a little, looking apologetic.

"Let's keep going and get something done," I say, "and then maybe I could take you out to lunch?"

She starts, unsure what to do.

"You look like no one's ever asked you out for lunch before," I point out then suddenly I boom with laughter. "You don't have to if you think it'd be 'inappropriate'. I just thought it might be fun, I'm a fun kind of guy."

Perhaps she'll think that sounds creepy or like a synonym for something but it's true, so I shrug easily and so does she. Then she dismissively replies, "I'll choose the place."

I take this as a success and feel rather pleased with myself, despite the banter I'll have to endure from the guys.

ANGELICA: 2.6 minutes

Cleaning out my father's old office is something that I have put off as long as possible, but I know my mother will never do it and it will loom over us as much as if his tombstone were in the house. I sit in the impressive chair and let my eyes slide around the room, deciding what he would have wanted to do with all the paperwork. I know he wanted me to take over the firm but I've never even met with any of the clients and I won't graduate with a degree to practice law for another two years.

I remember the pride he used to take in his work, how perfectly everything is filed. I am about to erase one man's life. The files are alphabetical and I begin emptying them off the shelves. Behind rows M-N I find a rusty key and I know it must be to the desk. I had never seen him open that desk. I can remember sneaking into his office once when he was on a walk with my mother and trying to prise open the draws by sheer will. What I would have given for this key then to know the secrets of that man! Now the anticipation is different; discovering a dead man's secrets is far less satisfying but I check if the key fits and, when it does, I turn it till the draw springs open, as it no doubt has done so many times for my father. It is filled with carefully filed letters of thanks which I begin to examine; it does not surprise me that people would want to thank my father for his work. He had once been the best in Munich. But as I rifle through phrases such as "I owe my family's safety to you" and "You have outdone your kindness and I can never repay you", I look closer at the clients' names and then search through the other drawers. I match the names to their files and this is when I find that all the letter writers are Jewish. I freeze, realization stinging my eyes. My father had been helping all his Jewish clients out of Germany throughout the war and the tears explode through me. As I collapse to the floor, clutching the letters, I am hit afresh with admiration and love for my father. He never even told my mother. He kept this selflessness, this burden entirely to himself.

I suddenly understand his outrage that one time I had questioned him about the Jews. Any suspicion raised could have been deadly and this only restarts the tears that won't quell and I don't try. I need to cleanse myself from this and this is the only way I know how. There is so much I want to ask him, want to tell him. I feel intensely guilty for my strained way of talking to him on his return home but I am selfish in a way that he never was and I couldn't be there for him the way he was there for so many. I feel so inferior and desolate that I just lie there with my dress spread in a pool around me, thinking of him until the light changes, then I pore over every letter, every detail and remember every compliment so that when I think or talk of my father it will be these things I tell.

When I am fully purged, I collect up the mess of documents and put them in order, then leave them on the kitchen table for my mother. I truthfully want to keep them to myself, my own last private connection to my father, but for his memory's sake she also has to see. But I don't want to share this experience with her so instead I grab my coat and leave to find the one living person who I want to share this with. I go to Jack's.

SABINA: 2.5 minutes

I'm sitting in the canteen waiting to meet Molly and, as always, the food is inedible so I get another hot water to pass the time. On my way back to the table I narrowly miss a collision with a bubbly girl in the year above which sets me thinking how strange it is that single moments can turn fate. If I had spilt the scalding water on her, she may have been burnt for life. It may have left her with ugly scar tissue, I may have been expelled and we both probably would have replayed the moment of collision in our minds. If only I'd turned, if only she'd seen me. Something that would have otherwise been inconsequential will be replayed in someone's mind, consistently trying to alter the scene, but as nothing happened this time we both pass by another moment without thinking on it.

Molly snaps me out of my dwelling suddenly. "You didn't tell me we were having lunch with her." Mona is halfway through stealing Molly's potatoes and rolls her eyes.

"I'm not thrilled by this new collaboration either."

"Is that your word of the week?" Molly mutters.

"As a matter of fact, it is. I have a chart on my wall and it's going very well actually. I've already used it three times today."

Molly throws me a sidelong glance and cuts in with, "You see, I say that as a joke but you can't even tease her cos she's proud of it!'"

"Mona and I are organizing something," I grin, "and we thought you might be interested?"

Molly talks only to me ignoring Mona, "Organizing what?"

"Basics," Mona loudly interjects, clearly not comfortable with an attention divide that leaves her with the lesser share. "Bini says you're top of the class in maths. Is that true?"

Molly looks embarrassed and mumbles something.

"Don't be coy," Mona snaps. "I'm not asking in order to congratulate you, I'm asking because I need the information."

"She is," I assure her, then I take over, "but I know you really struggle with history and German and Mona gets annoyingly good marks in science."

Mona starts to clap her hands with glee. "So in the upcoming exams, I figured the best policy for all of us to pass is if Bini writes all three of our history and German papers, I do the science and you do all three of the maths; that way we only read up on our favorite subjects and we all sail through to next year."

Molly hesitates, but I can see a smile curling up her face.

I nudge her. "You know it's a good idea."

"As long as we don't get in trouble, I'm in."

And although Mona imitates her behind her back, I feel like this is progress between my friends.

The plan works flawlessly. The invigilators are dozy and bored and we take our seats next to each other at the back of the room. Once we're handed a paper, the invigilator has to immediately turn around and walk all the way back up the aisle which gives us ample time to switch the papers effortlessly and we all agree afterward that it livens up the exam process considerably. All three of us get top marks and I leave for the holidays on a roaring high.

Thanks to my parents working away from home most of the time, I manage to retain my good mood and I am almost content in cooking and cleaning throughout the day then disappearing when they come home and have work parties. Sometimes they stay away overnight which would be fine by me too if the huge house didn't seem to swallow me up on these occasions. I lie swamped by the large bed in a thick and seemingly endless darkness, convinced that I can hear rustling downstairs. After a few nights I have to sleep with the lights on because I can't bear the idea of not seeing my attacker. It takes me three nights to work up the courage to investigate the sounds and I only eventually do so because the noises increase. I swear I can hear howling, as if someone is in pain. With an enormous amount of bravery I grasp my step-father's guitar, in case it comes to a fight, and I begin a very slow descent toward the sounds, convinced that someone is waiting to violently kill me behind every corner.

I reach the kitchen and the light won't turn on. I can see a shape moving slightly in the corner so I scream and start swinging the guitar around wildly, hoping that it will catch them by accident and knock them out, giving me time to run. Instead I hear a panicked screech and I feel something fluffy against my foot. As my eyes grow accustomed to the semi-darkness, I realize that it's a fat ginger cat and it's howling. My attitude changes instantly and I kneel down, abandoning the guitar and adopting a soothing voice. I tentatively reach out a hand to stoke it, not knowing if it is feral or not, and my hand comes away damp.

"What's the matter with you?" I coo as the cat slowly hobbles back toward the laundry basket and begins to rearrange the clothes, slightly desperately. At first I laugh, taking this as an insult to my washing but then the howling intensifies and I panic and try to fix the light. Once I can see that she is giving birth, I instantly leap in to action. I stroke her head, gently trying to soothe her, and fetch her a saucer of water. I sit with her, not knowing what I can do to make it better.

The first kitten arrives in a sort of pink sack and she instinctually begins to lick its face to break the membrane clear from the airways. I watch fascinated and mildly disgusted as she then proceeds to chew through a fleshy cord that this tiny cat is attached to. There is a round pile of flesh and goo on the end of it which, to my horror, she begins to eat. I stare at her in disbelief, questioning her judgment there, but halfway through this obscure display another kitten comes. While she is tending to that one, the first new-born is blindly pulling itself towards her milk, making pitiful mewing sounds. I giggle with relief when it finally latches itself on happily. After the third kitten she is exhausted, and although another kitten is coming she just lies on her back, panting, her eyes wide and desperate. I can see the fourth cat dying inside its little sack because it can't get any air. I hurriedly try and rub the sack clear of its nose but it is sticky and clings to it, like it's elasticated. I try harder and I see it open its mouth and bend its head, trying to help me. As soon as the head is clear, I can see it breathing and I gently peel the rest of the sac off its wet little heaving brand new body. I know I must now unattach it somehow from the lump of flesh it's connected to so I get a knife and run it under hot water, praying that this is the right thing to do and won't kill it. I kneel back down next to the little guy and gently stroke his head, lightly toughing his closed eyes. I take the knife and imagine that the cord is a piece of sailing rope from the boat house. I place the knife against it and slice through it in one clean sweep. I stare at the kitten, fearing its imminent death, but it doesn't even mew. I decide to tie the short cord that is still attached to it in a little bow to keep it out of its way, then I gently scoop him up and he fits in my hand perfectly. I place him with the others on his mother's teats, beaming with the release of tension and the success I feel. I scratch the ginger cat's forehead and she purrs softly... proudly... gratefully. I sit with the new family for the rest of the night.

The next day my parents return home and so I hide Ginger and her four babies with their laundry basket home in the cellar next to the boiler so that they will have enough warmth. I know that my parents would never let them stay and so I always creep down in the dead of night to tend to them. On the second night, as Ginger tucks into the leftovers I brought her, I notice the kittens' colorings as their fur has now dried and is fluffy. They are ginger but with odd black splotches, which are rather lovely, and I like the way the mum and dad's genes are so obviously displayed on a kitten. They're proudly, unavoidably marked and I mull over how much I am like my mother and real father.

On the third night I notice more movement in them. They will push each other blindly out the way and the smallest one always gets lost and I have to guide him back. At one week they begin to open their eyes and this is where the real beauty begins for them and for me, because they play and it is enchanting. They know nothing of the world or of pain or complexities, just their tiny happy family, and it warms my heart. I could watch them forever.

***

Sabina was allowed to enjoy the kittens for precisely one and a half weeks before there was a cruel intervention. I am going to tell this part of the story, partly because I don't like to re-watch the memory and partly because I can see both sides of it.

She awoke suddenly and was instantly confused for the alarm she set nightly to check on the Ginger and the kittens was not due to go off for another forty-five minutes. Then she started as something leapt onto her bed.

"Ginger!" she cried, scooping the cat up. "What are you doing? You're supposed to be with your kittens!"

Then she had frozen on the threshold of the door, trapped by foreboding. She whispered, "How did you get out?"

She placed the clearly-distressed cat on the floor and crept down the bleakly-lit hallway, beginning to hear the sound of running water. He was bent over the bath tub with his sleeves rolled up and laughing manically, turning his head dramatically when he noticed her in the doorway. His eyes were alight with alcohol and exhilaration and there was steam rising all around him.

"Sabina!" he boomed, barely able to speak through the laughter. "So glad you could join the fun!"

He ground his bare feet down into the broken glass of a bottle on the floor and threw his head back as a sound of pleasure ripped through him. She saw the mad tears running down his cheeks through the hysterics, and then her eyes fell onto the contents of the bath tub. He was holding a brown sack under the water and the sack was moving.

"Stop!" she shrieked. "Stop it, you'll kill them!"

"That is what I'm trying to do!" he bellowed back, terrifyingly.

If little Sabina could have seen Clemence all those years ago at the Hitler youth, rotting in his own filth, perhaps she could have laughed at him. Perhaps she could have thought him pathetic but at that moment he was terrifying and powerful and all she could do was watch, horrified, as he drowned all her kittens.

* * *

I shut the book, reeling from the horror of the last scene, and imaging the little girl as Lisa, helplessly screaming. I am also, however, enjoying the revelation. I have wanted the stories to intertwine for some time now and I muse over Clemence being Sabina's step-father. So this means that I am privy to his younger memories currently but now can also see what he becomes through her eyes. I shudder, flicking back to the last memory of his I read; he was getting drunk in some bar and hoping for something better. It seems that never came. I wonder who he marries and why they'd marry him, and who Sabina's actual father is. I force myself not to flick ahead in the book. Also I have work to do. I must stop being so preoccupied with fictitious characters and focus on reality.

I check the emails and to my great surprise, as there has been a lull in responses and the ones I have had have been unappealing, there is a promising looking email in my inbox. I open it, quickly feeling ridiculously excited considering I don't know what it contains. The content is straight forward and the images of their building grand. They want to see me for an interview next week but the exact position is unclear. It reads, 'To be determined at a later date' and that they prefer to 'See whether you're right for this company first'. This ethos appeals and I quickly reply a polite acceptance. After gladly mulling over what sort of things they will probably want to talk about, I decide to reward my success with a few more 'minutes'.

I open the book, now as fueled by the puzzle pieces to solve as their mysterious collector had been.

* * *

LOUISE: 1.7 minutes

I arrange my napkin on my lap carefully and then my hat while waiting for him to return from the toilet. I avert my gaze swiftly from making eye contact with other customers as it entails trivial responsibility. I'm nervous and I'm not entirely sure why. I try and calm myself by focusing on the words printed along the café walls. They frame a large mirror which reflects most of the room. I'm mulling over the word 'espresso', enjoying how saying it is as rich and soft as the drink itself, when I realize all the words are Italian and I begin to fret that it might be a sign.

"You talking to yourself?" he booms, bouncing back into his chair.

"I hadn't realized I was saying it out loud."

"That's okay, I'd rather you were crazy than dull."

He is rounded but it is attractive on him. I think it shows a love for good food, for life, so unlike most of the sickly, skinny men I am mostly forced into contact with. I adjust my hat again, trying to think of something to say to him, and I am very conscious that he won't go along easily with polite conversation. This leaves me lost as that is the only type I'm practiced in.

Without warning, he snatches the hat of my head and tries it on himself, adjusting it in the mirror.

"What are you doing?" I hurriedly protest, "give it back."

People are beginning to eye us warily. He dodges me swiftly.

"I'm sorry, is this annoying?" he trills, fiddling with the bow. "It is annoying to me too when you pay more attention to the damn hat than to me, the human being in front of you, willing to listen to you. Porrco vacca!"

It is the swearing in public, albeit in Italian, that forces me to storm out the door. I'm both furious and I want to laugh, but the two emotions conflict within me, confusing me as I search for a taxi home.

"I'm joking!"

I can hear his voice echoing behind me on the other side of the street but I keep walking.

"If you want your hat back you're going to have to stop."

"I don't get your sense of humor," I retort in a quieter tone so that no one thinks I'm the one who is trying to make a scene.

"I think you do, you just don't know how to deal with the fact that you do. But it's funny."

"I just thought you'd be more mature or educated or... I know you read Shakespeare, you quoted it to me!"

He laughs. "Yes, yes, this is Shakespeare! Shakespeare was not about being educated – he wrote it for the groundlings! It's about life, not gentlemen!"

I shake my head, "You wouldn't understand," I begin to laugh. "Yes, you would interpret it that way with your Italian 'life and passion' obsession."

"Shakespeare was Italian!" he bellows, practically dancing in front of me.

This throws me into hysterics for some unknown reason.

"Shakespeare was British so to say anything else is moronic. You're insulting to the bard. You're insane!"

"You read it through your lovely rose-tinted spectacles. I'm telling you he had a mutual love affair with Italy!"

"He's Britain's most celebrated writer!"

"Where are the best plays set? *Romeo and Juliet*! *Much Ado About Nothing*! *Two Gentlemen of VERONA*! *The Merchant of VENICE*!... Capirmi?"

He's fully fighting me now, holding nothing back, and it's rather exhilarating and equally infuriating.

"I don't know how I liked you so much in that opera!" The words slip out in the haze of emotion and suddenly he kisses me, right on the lips, in the middle of a crowded street with no hint of my permission beforehand. I slap him hard, out of panic and fury. It is not how I envisioned being kissed for the first time. Maybe I'm in shock but I turn decidedly and walk away. I look back briefly before turning into the next street and see him beginning to laugh wholeheartedly and pocketing my hat. I shake my head, dismayed. The only phrase I can think of to describe this insane man is 'er nimm ein blatt vor den mund'. It doesn't translate as well but fits him perfectly: 'he doesn't know how to put a piece of paper over his mouth'. He should learn to think before he speaks! I had to.

***

I liked Rita and had her memories been more relevant, I would have added them to this collection but then I am always drawn to unrequited love, if that is how you can describe the experiences of the next characters we see. In my eyes they are both unloved.

"I bought flowers," Hannis sang as he burst into Rita's house on one of his regular Saturday visits. She had got the cook to do a cheesecake, in case he visited, as she knew it was his favourite. She couldn't deny having a fondness for the boy that sometimes stretched to romantic fantasy, despite knowing she would never act on this.

"I daren't ask... I'm sure there are lots of girls." Rita walked him to the end of the pier and sat with him on the wooden bench that overlooked the whole of the lake. The reeds were high around them. "I know for a fact that everyone at the boating club is interested in you," she stated proudly, pulling on his cheek, "perhaps even some of the men." She chuckled darkly.

"You are terrible Rita! This cake, however, is not!" he exclaimed, shoveling down another mouthful.

"Well you know what they say, the way to a man's heart is through his stomach."

"Yup," he grinned, "simple creatures aren't we?"

She nodded in agreement. "Yes, but rather sweet... sort of like dogs."

He laughed amiably again. "I bet you had them all heeling and rolling over in your day!"

She laughed too. "Ah yes, I did… and not just figuratively." He grinned. "but that was a long time ago."

She sighed softly and a glint of the past glory seemed to flicker and die simultaneously within her.

"So let's focus on you," she suddenly stated, all business-like. "Which girl do you have your eye on?"

He grimaced. "The only one who doesn't seem to have eyes for me."

She gasps in mock horror. "No, she is immune to this," she gestures grandly at him, "charm?"

"You may laugh but I've been told I can charm anyone and I pride myself on it! Girls in general are not a problem for me."

"Explain the situation to me and I'll impart my years of wisdom."

When he was done, she nodded slowly. "This Angie, it seems you've simply been trying to woo her for too long. You must just simply be you with her before she can realize she wants to be with you. Go out with them as friends, have fun, stop fretting, and she will come to you."

The sun was beginning to set gently now and a silhouette of two fishermen could be seen in the distance, looking like a piece of Chinese fine art work. He walked her back up, past the boathouse and to the large house on the hill, laughing and talking of lighter things. At the door he thanked her with a sincere hug and then kissed her once, lingeringly on the lips, and left.

The sadness that this moment ignites within me for some reason is unbearable, so now I focus on the love. The Christmas Angelica decided to stay with Jack was one of the best Christmases she'd ever had. His family was one of the richest in the area, but like Jack, the only way their attitude reflected this was in their easy manner and laidback approach to life.

ANGELICA: 2.9 minutes

He had an older sister, Myrtle, whom everyone called Mad Myrtle as she was constantly coming up with new life plans, each of which was more outrageous then the last. She entertained us through lunch by discussing her latest exploits and her hopes to become a lion tamer while her parents rolled their eyes and Jack flipped between encouragement and teasing and was repeatedly stopped from butting in by her throwing her hand across his mouth. She was such a fascinating creature that I couldn't even judge her on her plain looks. I normally compared the woman around me to myself on a strict scale of attractiveness, always ensuring that I am the best-looking in a room when I enter.

I suppose his mother had won me over entirely on our first meeting by gushing, 'God you're so beautiful, even more so then Jack described.' He had winked at me behind her shoulder. The only exception was a grumpy old uncle who barely moved from the rocking chair and although I never saw him relight a cigar, he always seemed to be smoking one. This actually added to my enjoyment though, as every time Jack passed by him he would imitate him precisely, which made me and the rest of the family try not to laugh and the uncle repeatedly muse, 'What is the joke?'

We are lying in the snow on our backs looking up at the stars as he tells me all of their Christmas disaster stories and then, for no other reason apart from the fact that I want him to know, I tell him about my recurring ice dream where I must choose who will survive between the frozen people. He is flattered and fascinated that it now includes him, rather than judgmental.

"I find recurring dreams interesting," he says.

"You would!" I laugh, then I look at him. "Do you get any?"

"Well, if you don't find this kind of thing interesting, there's no need to tell you about my dreams."

"True," I say, "and I don't believe dreams mean anything."

But I want to know, to be privy to the inner workings of his mind, no matter how trivial, because I want to know him body and soul.

"You're going to tell me eventually anyway, whether I like it or not, so you may as well tell me now," I state.

"Is that so?"

I leap up and pull the blanket off the ground with me. "Wait, tell me inside."

"Picky tonight, are we?"

"No, I'm just freezing."

He gets up and rubs my arms quickly. "Yeah, your lips are going a bit blue actually."

"Warm them up then."

He obliges unquestioningly and I cling to him. I have never thought of myself as dependent on anyone but I know I could be with him. It's easy, like floating. Before this, every day was more like swimming against a gushing current.

Once we are on his bed, curled up together, I ask him again about his dream again.

"It's no way near as profound as yours, it's just odd."

"Like you," I tease.

"You want to hear it or not, cos don't push your luck."

"I promise to be captivated." He plays with my hair absently as he talks and it soothes me. "Well, I'm on the top deck of this open air boat at night, looking for a seat. There are sun loungers lined around the sides, but these are all taken. The only seat left is one that is central, facing forwards and reclined. I take this seat and lean back, shutting my eyes, suddenly realizing – as is possible in dreams where knowledge and acceptance happen simultaneously – that I'm dead. The other passengers talk unaffectedly in low voices around me about trivial matters, the driver announces that we will be listening to Bob Marley, and then the boat begins travelling. The wind is refreshing through my hair and on my face, but after a while it begins to chill me. And everytime the music repeats itself it sounds increasingly insincere. I have this incessant feeling that it's not going to be all right at all, but as the song ends I wake up."

He stops and looks at me. I'm studying him, fascinated.

"I've never told anyone that before," he muses, "not that it's a big deal. I just like that no one else knows that, apart from you."

I smile, "I like that too, very much." I pause then look down. "I could tell you something too… that I've never told anyone."

He pulls my chin up so that I have to look at him.

"A dream?"

"Actually," I sigh, "it's sort of a fantasy."

I must be blushing, which never happens to me, because he touches my cheek gently and says, "You can tell me."

"You'll think it's really strange," I say "but, what excites me sometimes, is to imagine that I've been in an accident. Nothing fatal, just that I am knocked out for a few seconds by a car and the entire street stops and everyone crowds around, transfixed by me lying there.

There are ambulance sirens and doctors yelling at people to get back as they gently examine me and everything is out of my hands. I'm being taken care of by other people, I have their whole attention."

I pause, scared that he is going to laugh, but instead he slowly kisses my neck, pulling my hair back. He gently lays me back on the bed, he keeps eye contact with me as he gently lets his fingers trace over my leg as he brings it across the other one. His fingers tease open my blouse. Gently he traces my spine, sending tingles shooting through me, and I am gripped by desire.

"You have my whole, undivided attention." His voice is intense and sincere. He places my hand underneath my head. "Don't move," he whispers and then kisses me and our trembling bodies begin to fuse together. I know he is the only person I want to do this with.

It was the most erotic moment of my life.

* * *

The door slams and I look up. Sarah's home early. I get up to greet her and tell her the promising news of my interview, but as I enter the hallway I see her leaning against the wall, crying. I'm instantly disturbed and panicked; my wife is resilient in almost any situation. She sees me and runs to hug me, yelling, "My bloody mother!" The rest is lost in sobs.

I just hold her and gently guide her to the kitchen so the kids, who are playing outside, won't know she's back yet and see her in this state. I know that's the last thing she'd want.

"You won't believe this!" The wracking sobs are subsiding and anger is overtaking. "I only took that bloody job in the first place under the agreement that when she retired, the company gets passed down to me! Years of flying to Germany and working long hours and putting up with her and being away from you and missing my girls! And she throws it back in my face, and in front of everyone, I'm jobless! I quit! I wouldn't work another day for her. Oh God..."

She begins to cry again and I try to soothe her, hating her mother for doing this to us. I know that Sarah would have never taken the job if she hadn't thought that eventually she would be fully in control of her own income.

At that moment the girls come rushing in with shrieks of 'Mum!' and, in a panic, she gets up and locks herself in the bathroom. I try to distract them with fresh brazens she always brings back for them which they like heated up with butter and honey on the side to dunk them in, but they can sense that something's not right. After a while they hear the sobs coming from the bathroom.

I don't see this as an overreaction on Sarah's part. I know that this will make old memories resurface and make her feel stupid for trusting her Mum again. The girls both make 'Hope you feel better soon Mum' notes and slide them under the door. Eventually she comes out to hug them and tell them that nothing's really that bad and that she hoped she didn't scare them.

Later I try to comfort her with the news of the interview.

"God, I hope you get it," she says, holding my hand tightly. "How long can we last here with both of us unemployed?"

She rests her head against me, fatigue setting in, and I stroke her hair.

"It will be ok," I say, despite there being absolutely no guarantee of this. Maybe the book I'm reading has given me a belief in fate and, deep down, although the situation looks bleak, I have faith.

* * *

This next moment is somewhat of a turning point in Clemence's life. He rolled from the bed of Mrs. Stanzil hurriedly, having to hide in the wardrobe while her husband came in to wish her good morning. He calmly rolled a cigarette in the dark, cramped space and mulled over the interview he had lined up for the afternoon, wondering how to play it. He decided an all or nothing approach would be required.

"Because you need me," he booms, spreading his arms wide. He has sobered up and is ambitious for this business endeavor to work out. "I'm compelling, and when I need something to work, it does." He laughs easily, balancing his chair on its two back legs and rubbing his moustache, a gesture which he thinks rather adds to his image.

"You do realize that door to door selling is not glamorous?" the interviewer asks, shuffling the job application papers.

"I'm not interested in glamour, sir, only money."

The balding man sighs. "Well, your history in selling is good… according to you."

"Not just good, I'm outstanding."

There is a pause. "That may be so, my fresh-faced young man, but where is the proof? Where are your credentials? Recommendations? All I have is your word, and what's that worth?"

Clemence leans over the desk, resting his chin on his hands intently. "Are you telling me that you run this company without even a little trust in another man? In your own employees? You're going to look in to my eyes and tell me I'm lying just because I've got nothing backing up my word apart from my own conviction. How is an honest man supposed function if society is filled with people like you?"

The man chuckles. "You talk well, kid. I'll give you a trial period and make up my mind based on that. Satisfactory for you?'"

"Wonderful! It's a deal then," and he extends his hand across the desk with a ring master's showmanship.

SABINA: 2.6 minutes

My first memory is of sitting in a car, watching everything my dad owns go flying out the window of our flat, my mum pulling me out of the car and screaming at him. When I play this memory back, I imagine that my dad wanted to take me with him but my mum didn't want anybody to have me except her. I fantasize about running away to find my real dad a lot. I lie on my bed in the dorm, listening to 'Children of the Revolution' and imagine that my dad's looking for me too, and that when he finds me he'll whisk me away to a better life.

Today my dreams are cut short when Molly enters. I can see she is full and she barely makes it to my bed before she is in floods of tears. A girl whom I've never spoken to before, called Abigail, has found out about her mum and has been whispering snide comments such as 'Madness is hereditary' and 'Do you think she's actually mad or that she puts it on for attention?' for over two weeks.

"You should have told me sooner!" I say, hugging her.

"I thought she'd stop," she sniffles, "but it's getting worse!"

I hug her more tightly as I realize how fragile she is and this is a topic that runs deep. I know that there is nothing I can say to make it better but there is something I can do. And I know who to ask.

"We're talking the bigger the better here," she instructs as we pick our way across the fields round the school. "Okay, here's good," she says when we come across a dank leafy patch. I sprinkle the mashed up egg near a tree and we hide a couple of meters back in waiting.

"Is it true?" she asks and I look up at her, "about Mol's mum?"

I look away and nod. "Don't say anything to her."

"I won't... it makes her truly part of the club now anyway, right? All of our families are messed up." She is grinning but I'm not sure if I can share her mood. "There," she whispers.

I look and can make out a hedgehog sniffing around the leaves then finding the egg and munching away. We creep towards it stealthily and Mona expertly tips the box over it and scoops it up. I decide to add some leaves and the rest of the egg to keep it happy on the ride which makes Mona roll her eyes.

"How do you know this anyway?"

"At home we have to keep them away from the dogs because they carry so many fleas."

We scuttle through the school, darting in and out of rooms, making me feel like those cats you see on the edge of fish ponds who so desperately want the fish, but every time they go for it, their paws get wet and they retreat.

Mona keeps watch at the door while I let the hedgehog run wild in Abigail's sheets for a good ten minutes then scoop him back in to his box. I carefully follow Mona's instructions of gently rubbing its tummy as I scoop it up to stop it curling up and pricking me. We let him go outside where he scampers away from the crime.

That night, just before lights out, I whisper to Molly that Mona and I have taken care of it for her. Although her eyes widen, she looks pleased. The matron comes in and snaps at us to all get into bed, which we do. Then she gives us a short lecture on how next year will work and that as we approach the end of the first year, it is customary to give the teachers gifts. Throughout this there are intermittent rustling sounds from the corner of the room and then a small squeak.

The matron turns. "For heaven's sake girl, lie still!"

The lights are out and it is a strict rule that no one leaves their beds or is allowed to talk until we are called for in the morning, so we lie in silence listening to her scratching, panicked protest. I reach out my arm to Molly in the darkness and squeeze her hand. I know

Mona is doing the same on the other side and we fall asleep triumphantly.

The next morning Abigail leaps out of bed and yanks her sheets off the bed for washing. Her skin is covered in angry red bites and I know that this will drive her mad more due to looks then itching. Molly stares straight at her spotty face and then slowly sticks out her tongue. Abigail does not give her any more trouble.

***

I spend a lot of time on Sabina's pranks but they're my favorites. After all, a girl born from neglect and loneliness could do far more damage than perfecting the art of practical joking and I like to observe and dance around these lighter parts of her life as they have the effect of making me want to join in.

However, we now go to more adult issues: love and such. A puzzling concept, and in all my years on the job I have heard many different definitions of the phenomenon but one of my best belongs in this story and is Jack's definition. Angelica, in her need for a logical explanation to things, had questioned him on how you could explain the feeling of love and he had replied that love is like the biting point of a car's engine. You can't really explain it and it can only occur if everything is just right and people only really understand it when they're feeling it. I like that.

Anyway, in this case it is to do with Louise. Louise, pretentious or simply intelligent, shy or eccentric, is hard to place but she has a good soul and I like watching her journey so I'll put my musings to one side. The day she realized she was in love with the strange Greek man Mangos was when they went on an ill-advised sailing excursion.

LOUISE: 2.3 minutes

"Of course I can sail, I'm Greek!"

He had convinced me. We hired a catamaran, something I had never heard of, and he made me put on a harness too. I was sort of enjoying the way the whole thing worked with him yelling "Tack!" and then me having to scuttle across to the other side of the boat. He was more authoritative here, enjoying being the teacher for a change. Until he told me to clip myself on to the edge of the boat with the harness and lean back off it, I was hesitant, but he had promised I would enjoy it. It was fantastic. The waves hit repeatedly and the wind flung back my hair dramatically. I was alive and began to yell, thinking it was no wonder that they say Venus was born at sea.

I raised my arms and, at that moment, a particularly large wave knocked me off my feet and I felt myself flying, still attached to the boat, around the rudder, the rope getting caught up. I managed to grab hold of the other side of the boat. Mangos looked terrified. We were heading toward the shore and he tried to tack but the rope attached to me was caught around the mast so it wouldn't turn. As we picked up more and more speed, he was yelling, "Unclip the harness! Unclip it!" I tried but was laughing too hard. "Unclip yourself now!" I was doubled over at this point, tears streaming down my cheeks. The whole thing was brilliant – the air, the speed, his face!

Eventually I gathered myself enough to undo the rope and we turned, his face drained and staring at me.

"What was that, you crazy woman?" he asked but I merely laughed.

Mangos had finally met his match.

***

I like to observe people in love and their differing attitudes side by side as I often did with Angelica and Jack. Perhaps their differences cancelled each other's out, creating a balance? I do not know but merely by watching each in the memory of the other, I know 'it' worked.

"To lie down on the grass makes one a part of nature," he had yawned, sprawling out in the heat. Reluctantly she lay beside him. The problem was that she felt too much a part of nature. In her opinion, as soon as you lie on the grass the earth begins to claim you, the grass grows around you and the bugs start to feed. The ground reminds you that it will have you one day. He was oblivious to her fears with his eyes shut and his head tilted back toward the sun, enjoying the orange and red picture show on the inside of his eyelids.

ANGELICA: 3.2 minutes

"By the way, I said we'd go out with Hannis tonight," he says sleepily.

"What?" I groan back. "I just want it to be you and me."

"He is a mate of mine. Why can't the three of us all just hang out?"

I sigh, leaning my head on his body. He always seems to tremble slightly beneath me. I take a moment and try to get our breathing in sync.

"He was drunk last time, Angie. He's a good guy, I like him."

I raise my eyes to his. "Do you really?"

Jack was an excellent judge of character in my opinion and fairly picky about his close friends. I knew that lots of people wanted to be close to him, or even thought they were, but only a few actually shared mutual respect. I'd once teased him that before I knew him, I used to mockingly describe it like Jesus and his disciples – a bunch of bored men following a more impressive man with no particular evidence of a reason. This had got us started on a two-hour debate as he was more religious than me.

"I like to have faith in something tangible," I had said,

"That's fine," he'd assured me, "but it's important to have faith in something, anything."

To which I had replied that I had faith in him and, for me, that was enough.

"Well then, you're no better than a disciple."

"No, actually, I've based my devotion on carefully collected evidence"

He'd laughed and promised to put this 'devotion' to the test at some point.

We meet Hannis and some other girl in a bar that evening and he is back to his usual exuberant self. He slaps Jack on the back and they catch up while buying us drinks. The girl opposite me is averagely pretty and talkative and makes the kind of small talk I hate. The evening, however, is wonderful. Jack leaps through topics of conversation and Hannis tries to keep up and then, when we have exhausted our minds, someone suggests Pictionary. We play for the rest of the night in our half-drunken state, which makes the childish game endlessly entertaining. Jack and I beat Hannis and the girl (I can't remember her name). I think we win because our minds are on the same frequency. I'll have barely got past a squiggle when he'll yell out 'cat on a hot tin roof!' and there will be an uproar from the other two that we must be cheating somehow. But we just know how the other thinks.

SABINA: 2.8 minutes

The start of a new term very often means new teachers, and thanks to the school's attempt to broaden our horizons by involving more artistic subjects, we are introduced to the young Mr. Lapzel, our photography teacher. Almost all of the girls in our year instantly fall in love with him. He must be straight out of college and he is pale with piercing blue eyes that, admittedly, are rather hard to look away from. Me and Mona agree that he is far too 'pretty boyish' and so we refrain from joining in with the other girls' giggling circles of gossip and speculation as to whether or not he has a girlfriend, and if he was to date someone at this school who would be the most likely. Annoyingly, Molly is sucked into this cult and it is impossible to talk about anything else with her for the first term which becomes incredibly tedious and me and Mona try to plot ways to snap her out of this frenzied crush.

We have the lessons in a dark room, which bodes well for Molly and those who share her feelings, as once the lights are off their blushes are hidden from view. After a week of hearing Molly gush about how last lesson he touched her shoulder and complimented her on her progress, and her constant need for our opinions as to whether that meant that he was actually giving her a signal for something more, Mona was more blunt than me in pointing out the age gap and the wedding ring on his finger that all the other girls stated was merely a jewellery choice.

The plan is mean. I can't deny that but its brilliance grabs me and I can't resist going ahead with it. Mona is delighted. During lunch break both of us slip into the photography room and flick the lights on, Mr. Lapzel has hung our final prints on string all around the room. Hurriedly we both begin to unclip these and put them on people's desks instead, then we empty our bag and hang the knickers proudly across the room. There must be twenty pairs in all, all of which have MOLLY HILTZ printed across the label in bold. We are giggling ferociously the entire time and when the room is fully decorated, we both double over imagining his horrified expression when he enters the room and sees this as a rather forward advance from one of his twelve-year-old students. We switch the lights off and then, filled with anticipation, sneak out.

We had chosen a day when photography was our first lesson after lunch and everyone spills into the classroom excitedly, awaiting to see their finished prints and pondering over whose he'll like the best. Mr. Lapzel enters a few minutes after and, as always, switches on the lights to begin the class. Now here is a moment worth being captured in a photograph. It lasted a couple of seconds too long as everyone's eyes adjust to the bright light, then the nervous titters start as everyone turns to stare at Molly, the red spreading across her face like ink dropped in water. Slowly Mr. Lapzel also looks straight at her in slight awkwardness and shock. It is hilarious; he has no idea what to do next. She has no idea what to do next either. He walks slowly to the front of the room, ducking carefully under the rows of pants, and taps his desk.

"What is this?" he says, looking distressed. "Molly?"

Suddenly unable to take it anymore, she leaps up and begins ripping the pants down as if everyone will instantly forget that they had once been hanging there.

He stares at her, puzzled.

"I'm not sure what that was..." he trails off then he laughs a little, "but just in case... I want to tell you all that I'm a married man."

Molly flushes more intensely, hiding the pile of pants under her jumper. He avoids eye contact with her for the rest of the lesson and she sits very still while the rest of us are distracted the entire lesson by reliving the event and intermittently cracking up with laughter.

I begin to wonder if I had sacrificed my friendship for this one gag and if so, I definitely should have caught it on camera. I do feel a little guilty but in the long run, I know this will make things better. Besides, by the end of the lesson Mr. Lapzel has gathered himself together and assures Molly that he will not report this incident to the Principal and that he is sure she meant it as a joke and nothing more. And he is actually exactly right.

ANGELICA: 3.5 minutes

The sun is low in the sky and so I pull down the shield on his side.

"How close are they behind us?" he asks, his eyes focused on the road ahead.

"No one's in view," I say beaming, "we've got this. We take the left up ahead and then it's one mile till victory!"

He spins the car round the bend and I smile, loving the sudden shot of excitement. I glance down at the map; business before pleasure. We need this race.

"Okay, we need to turn round that big rock formation up ahead."

I feel the car jerk to the side.

"Not yet," I hit his helmet, "up ahead."

The car jerks again.

"Where?" he stammers.

"What's the matter with you? I said it twice, we..." but I am cut of as the car slides off the road and we begin to veer crazily down the side of the hill. I'm screaming at him to stop and bracing myself against the door but the speed continues to increase. "Jack!"

I look over at him, terrified, but his arms are shaking wildly and he doesn't look like he can hear me.

"Jack!" I yell again, desperately.

I lean over and grab the wheel, knowing that his foot is jammed on the accelerator, and that is when I see the river stretching ahead with no visible way to steer around it. I know this is it. I grab Jack's unresponsive hand and pray for the first time in my life.

The car plunges into the water and everything is instantly dark but I can feel the downwards motion rapidly. Water begins gushing in at my feet. I don't know which way is up or down. All I can feel is fear. I begin kicking the sun roof out, screaming as I do so, then it cracks and I am instantly covered in glass and water. Panicking, I kick off the seat and fight my way to what I hope and pray is the surface, my lungs tight with the possibility that they have already felt their very last air. I hear a gagging from deep within me and then I see light. I surface and gulp in the air, then I know that he will not have been able to get himself out.

Without hesitation I dive back under. I kick with new found strength and purpose. For a terrible second I think I can't see the car anymore, but soon I make out a black shape and I lunge at it, anger fuelling me. I reach through the sun roof and grab his jacket. I yank him through and see that the glass cuts his cheek as I pull him out but I can't think on that now. I drag him to the surface, willing him to see light and air again. I don't know how I get his limp form on to the bank but I do.

I start compressions frantically, unable to remember how many to do. 1, 2, 3, 4, trying to force the life back into him. 5, 6, 7, 8, 9, 10, my own breaths rasp, willing him to join me. 11, 12, 13, 14, I stop pressing methodically, the panic taking over, and I begin to hit him wildly. Suddenly I am furious, illogically furious, at him and I begin to spit and swear as I return to compressions. What else can I do?

"Don't die! Wake up! Bastard! Talk to me! Open your eyes now!" I stop suddenly staring rigidly at his face. 'No,' is all I can think. This. Can't. Happen.

"Mouth to mouth," my mind screams. I haven't tried that yet and I know why: kiss of life? What if it doesn't work? What if it is the kiss of death? What if I can't save him?

I slam my hands either side of his head, pinch his nose and calmly breathe into his mouth. Once. Twice. Nothing. And that is when I rock back on to my knees and scream.

"Shut up," he groans, coughing up water and mucus, and I leap on him but he falls back laughing a little. I sit behind him and pull him up into me. I'm shaking in shock.

"What happened?" I ask, kissing him on the cheek. He is still coughing and trying to pull himself up but I hold him there.

"You think we could still get back in the race?"

I lean my head against his my cheek pushed against his wet hair.

"Sure," I mumble against him, "if we still had a car."

And we are silent for a moment, savouring our escape and being terrified of it, all at the same time.

HANNIS: 3.6 minutes

"Is that you?" I croon, grabbing a photo off the mantelpiece. The weather is bad today and so we cannot sit as she would have liked down on the jetty by the boats house. I've never stayed long in Rita's house before and now I discover it is treasure trove of the past.

"Yes, and that is my husband next to me." I bring the photograph over to her.

"Well Rita, you did well for yourself."

She laughs in her throaty old way and agrees. "He was very charming and very handsome."

"Were you in love?"

She muses. "I suppose. It's hard to tell really. We were a very good couple. My mother hated him, and in my experience you'd make an excellent couple with anyone your mother hates."

I smile, staring at the young couple. "You stayed together though, until..."

"Yes, yes. 'Till death do us part' meant more in those days. No children. I would have loved children... Franklin always said our kind of lifestyle didn't accommodate them but I think he just didn't want to see me get fat."

She laughs again. "Could you get me a cigarette, Hannis?"

"You don't smoke."

"I've started smoking. I'm dying anyway, my dear, so now it really doesn't matter if I smoke or not. So goddamn it, I will!"

Laughing I hold up my hands in surrender. Finding a packet in one of the drawers, I set it up for her. She puffs away with grace and mild coughs, but the overall image is striking rather than disgusting.

"How could you not know if it was love or not? I mean, I think I am a romantic at heart. I've loved one woman for my entire life and one day I'll marry her."

"What makes you love her?"

I pause. "Everything!"

Rita nods. "Often I find that people fall for an idea of love. Perhaps love is an invention that we all have convinced ourselves exists. It is fairly difficult... I would venture impossible to spend your life with another human being and always love them."

"But you and Franklin... I have to believe that it is possible, that not everything falls apart!"

I can hear the slight anger in my voice and know I'm referring to my parents problems. She knows it is something that is rooted deep within me and has had a far greater effect than I let on. She smiles gently and rearranges herself in her seat.

"I have a proposition for you. I know things at home are not good, so I am asking you if you could like to move into the boats house. Your own place. I know it is small and would need some cleaning and yes, I refer to it as 'sheiz house', but... it is an escape, yes? You could even bring your girl there."

Smiling I raise my eyebrows. "Oh Rita, das sheiz house? I couldn't possibly!"

We both begin to laugh.

LOUISE: 3 minutes

It is one of those clumsy conversations where nothing is said for far too long and as soon as a new topic evolves, you both talk at rapid speeds, tripping over each other's points with your own. I have a theory that this shows the impatience of both parties because if they attempted talking at an average velocity, and letting the other person finish their sentence, then a continuous conversation would prevail.

I had known that introducing him to my parents would not go smoothly; he seems to represent another world altogether and in their eyes this is perceived as danger. They have spent too much on my education for me to come by any harm now.

I keep quiet, much to everyone's annoyance, as both parties want me to back up their points. Mangos wants me to come to Freiberg with him when the opera leaves Britain. I have agreed on the condition that my parents allow it. I am very taken with Mangos. He has captivated me, made me argue, made me laugh, but I am not entirely convinced about moving to a country I've never been in my life with no one I know besides him. Wonderful, admirable, unpredictable: no one word will really suffice. He cannot be summed up.

I am desperately hoping they'll say yes while also begging them to forbid it.

"Out of the question," my father snaps.

"You are not married, not even engaged!" my mother agrees. "We are in discussion with a lovely gentleman's parents at the moment. They are interested in an engagement between our children which could not possibly go ahead if she were in Germany!"

"And what of your studies? You have not finished your teaching qualification yet."

"It will only be for a year," he assures them. "I make a very good amount of money at the moment. I can fund the rest of her course in Germany, then bring her back in one piece after a year."

He tries to throw in a confident wink but my mother cuts him off with, "After you've ruined her!"

"I warned you," I mutter to him under my breath,

"Fine! I came prepared for this possibility." He throws back his chair with his kamikaze energy. It scrapes along the floor and topples, over making my parents gasp. Then he falls to one knee and whips out a ring.

"Louise, will you marry me?"

It is not the stuff of romance novels and neither of us is heroic or particularly beautiful but I am rather taken with the display and know that violins or a stroll along the beach would have made me cringe. My parents' shocked and horrified expressions add to my amusement and I very happily say "Yes." It's odd to think this, but perhaps if my parents were being more reasonable the answer would have been different. The fear would have won rather than the freedom.

* * *

Sarah's offered to take the kids to work so I can make sure that I won't be late for my interview. I pull up next to a glass building, which is elaborate to say the least, and I recognize it from the website as well. There is a large sign: Archive of historic and Current Arts. I begin to get excited.

I get out of the car and begin to walk toward the door glancing at my reflection in a vehicle's window and straightening my unfamiliar tie, only to notice there is a man in the car glaring back at me. I try to laugh it off but he continues to glare, so I shrug and walk toward the entrance, feeling unwelcome already.

The foyer is lavish and I try not to look like a lost boy as I helplessly gaze at the chandeliers which drip from the ceiling.

"Can I help you?" a curt receptionist asks. She has a slight accent, French or Russian perhaps.

"Yes, I'm here for an interview," I state. She smooths one side of her pristinely tied back hair and narrows her eyes. "There are no interviews today."

I stare at her, feeling embarrassed though I haven't done anything wrong.

"Sorry, I was under the impression... I got an email for an interview today. My name is William Tief."

She looks up again, having ignored me until that point.

"Oh," she says carelessly, "yes, they're holding interviews in the outbuilding."

She gives me directions impatiently and then I gladly leave the foyer. I'm not really sure I want to work at this place but I dutifully follow the instructions and find myself confronted with a shabby wooden structure hidden by the rest of the building. Although it, too, is large, it is the exact antithesis of the place I have just left. It is almost as if someone has built the structure hurriedly and doesn't expect it to last more than today.

Inside there are multiple corridors and rooms and I am greeted warmly by an old man who gives me a seat and asks me to fill out a questionnaire while I wait. I sigh, knowing I am going to have to scrawl down all of the trivial information about myself, so I settle down in the chair, resting my foot on my knee to make a sort of table and then turn the paper over. I get through, name, age, sex and status easily but I am caught slightly off guard by the next question: 'Describe the room you are sitting in.'

I look up, smiling, hoping there will be someone to laugh about this with, but I'm alone so I set about completing this task. After I have done that I move on to a picture question. There is an image of an old man on a bench in a park alone, staring up. 'What does this image say to you?' This seems more relevant and I talk of the contemplation of life and other things that speak to me.

I move on to the next questions. 'What do you value?'; 'If you could do anything with your life, what would it be?; 'What are you currently reading?'; 'What do you think of it?'

It is the most impractical questionnaire I have ever filled in for a job interview but I quite enjoy it. For the last two questions I use an old favorite, *Of Mice and Men* instead of the Seven Minutes book I am actually reading, because I can't for the life of me remember who wrote it.

At that moment I am shown into a cozy but bright office and a friendly, spindly man named Billy Smith takes my form from me. He settles into the chair behind the desk and reads through it.

"Great, take a seat," he says when he looks up. "Good to meet you, Will. We just have a few questions for you today. You work in the history of art sector?"

"Yes, that's correct," I say, ready to launch into my spiel of where I studied, how my old company closed down, but I am cut off.

"Great. And can you tell me what is it you like about history of art?"

I pause, "The story behind a picture, I think. You know it's this one moment in time and you can interpret the before and after, and why the people in the picture are as they are. But also how the artist was when he painted it – why and what he was feeling at that moment. It's basically just the coming together of many stories in one frozen moment."

"Great. Are all your answers true on this questionnaire?"

I laugh nervously, "Uh, well I'm reading this other book but I can't remember the name of the author so I just put down one of my other favorites."

"Great. Are you afraid to die?"

"What? Uh yeah, I guess every body's afraid to die."

"Let's talk about that.'

'Sorry, what does this have to do with the interview?"

"We are very interested in your views on all aspects of life. What do you think of people who kill themselves?"

"What is this position for?" I ask firmly.

Billy Smith sighs as though bored, "We will require you to be able to write descriptive, informative captions for the pieces we receive. Does that sound like something that would interest you?"

"Yes, actually, that sounds fascinating. What kind of pieces do you mostly deal with?"

He seems uninterested in my response and proceeds with his own,

"Great. Are you loyal to your job?"

"Yes."

"Great, well it was lovely to meet you Will, take care."

"Did I get the job?" I ask, feeling that the whole thing has been a bit of a blur,

Billy Smith smiles, "I'll have to ask my superiors, and really, only time will tell."

And with that the whole affair ends and I am left a little baffled. I drive home disgruntled and agitated, feeling a bit like a fool. At home I quickly remove the uncomfortable tie and trousers and shroud myself in the comfort and familiarity of well worn jeans and tend to the animals to distract my disappointed thoughts. After that I return to the lounge, wanting to tell Sarah about the strangeness of the day, but she is at a meeting with a company she has done some freelance work for in the past, so I retrieve the book as a source of company instead.

* * *

CLEMENCE: 3 minutes

I am very good at developing formulae. It's how I learnt to charm women years ago and how I taught myself to sell. After each sale I do, I mentally review my work, what helped and what hindered, and then I simply reuse the good stuff until I have perfected the art. There's a reason I have the highest sales rates on the team. The company has stationed me in Munich and at one of the houses I go to this morning with my cart of typewriters, I am greeted by a woman who looks at me cautiously, half hidden behind the door. I pick up on her nerves instantly. It is important to observe the potential buyer's body language and adjust yourself accordingly.

I look down bashfully and open with, "I'm sorry to bother you but I have a very interesting product here that I'd like to discuss with you."

She glances at the cart behind me.

"What is it?"

"State of the art typewriters," I say in awe. "They are really cutting edge and they're selling like wild fire." I look back at the cart longingly. "If I had the money, I'd have got one by now. Can I show you how it works?" I ask eagerly.

She smiles a little and steps outside her door. "Go on then."

I dart back to the cart and bring one up.

"Here, have a go if you like," I say, knowing not to be too forceful but to always give the customer the option.

I set it up and she types a little.

"The keys are all incredibly smooth," I go on, "and the carriage returns easily too, you see?"

A little kid runs toward the door then, yelling "Mummy, what's for lunch?"

She tells him to wait inside and I take this as a piece of potentially useful information as I begin to focus on closing the sale.

"It is rather lovely," she agrees.

"The best part is that it's totally portable and comes with this smart case. You can use it anywhere."

She examines the case. "I just don't know how much I'd use it."

"Well," I say, "I'm sure it would be useful for your son to do his homework on and it's a great skill now to be able to type. You could teach him!" She looks fairly taken by this idea. "So would you like to buy?" and yet another sale is complete. I deal with a grumpy old man later who has his arms gruffly folded throughout our entire conversation; defensive. I glance down his hallway and see a picture of him and a woman at a church.

"Whatever you're selling, I'm not buying."

"Well now, you can't possibly make an informed decision without having tried the product." I hand him the typewriter and launch into my rehearsed reasons as to why it's good: -portable, smooth carriage, takes any type of paper.

"Why would I need this?" He shakes his head.

"No, you're quite right" I say without missing a beat, "You may not need this but it is an excellent product, and it would make a wonderful gift, maybe for someone in your family, a wife perhaps?" He shrugs and looks down at the typewriter.

"Well, no rush," I say, "I've got to come back this way anyway. I could drop by then? Tell you what you could hold on to that one until I get back? Think of it like a trial. That way you can thoroughly examine and test it."

People like him love this; it makes them think they've won like they're controlling you or have some hold over you now. He agrees.

I visit all of the other houses on the street and only one person refuses to buy and that is purely down to price. I then find myself in a back street and decide to try my luck here too although the area does not look as rich. I ring the doorbell of the first house, and this is where I meet Hildi. A curvaceous young woman answers it, her hair is dark brown and done up scrappily on top of her head with a scrunchie and she is holding a wooden spoon covered in cake mixture in her hand. She notices it dripping on the floor and quickly licks the remnants off the spoon while asking, "Can I help?"

She does not look like the kind of woman who would have the use for a typewriter. Her breasts are practically spilling out of the tight top she is wearing and her shorts squeeze her thighs appealingly.

"I'm selling type writers" I say, "can I come in?"

"Sure, ok," she chirps, hopping out the way. She had a bouncy walk and she leads my into the kitchen where she continues mixing her cake. Some song by Chuck Berry is playing quietly in the background and she moves in time to the music. I set the typewriter on the desk and I explain it to her and she smiles and nods openly.

"You want to try it?" I pat my knee and she nods, skipping over and perching on my lap. "You just type like this," I say letting my fingers push down on the keys. I and write, 'I think you're very attractive'.

She smiles at the words and types back, 'So are you.'

It is cliché and simple but quite cute I suppose. It reflects her personality. Somehow we begin to dance to the music and it's not long before I have pushed her down onto the sofa. Her lips are sweet due to the cake mix. I rip her top off and she undoes my belt hungrily. She is one of those women who is loud and unthinking and I like that when it is purely for animalistic pleasure rather than when the other person is thinking things. Hildi does not have this problem. We both yell out and are aggressive and I thoroughly enjoy myself.

I thank her before I leave and, on my way home, finish my sale with the grumpy man and collect my money. If you stick to what you're good at, there's no reason why you can't be a success.

ANGELICA: 3.8 minutes

I tap my foot nervously in the Hospital waiting room. His mum is also here as she was the one who insisted after the accident that they run tests to see if there is anything wrong. I'm clutching his jacket which he casually threw to me when they called him to be seen.

"I'm sure everything's fine," his mum tries and I nod.

"For sure," I agree, but I can't get the image of him unable to stop shaking in the car out of my mind.

I bring the jacket surreptitiously up to my face, pretending I'm cold but actually wanting to inhale his smell to calm me. I try to focus on other things – my finals coming up, the revision I still need to do – but every time someone walks down the hall, my head shoots up expectantly.

Finally he enters and I leap up towards him. He is standing casually and I am struck anew, as I always am when we're in a crowded place, by how much he stands out as an attractive presence. I give him his jacket and wrap my arms around him.

"You ok?" I whisper, and he nods but his shoulders are tense beneath my fingers. A doctor's voice cuts in then.

"Are you Mrs Cultz?"

I say "yes" at the same time Jack's mother does. They all look at me and I blush, pretending not to have said anything. Of course he was talking to Jack's mum. Jack is still staring at me and gently links our hands.

"Could I possibly have a word with you in private?" says the doctor.

Jack's mum nods.

"Should I come too?" I ask.

The doctor looks at Jack and his mum for approval. She puts her arm around me.

"For heaven's sake, let's all go."

But Jack grimaces. "I think I'll wait outside," he says, letting go of my hand and sliding his jacket on as he pushes through the doors.

We sit in a tiny room with only one chair so I have to perch on the examination bed. The walls are grimly white-washed and the room smells painfully clean, as if someone is trying to hide another stench, and it makes my jaw clench.

"Your son has been diagnosed with MS," the doctor begins.

I'm not entirely sure what this means so I am unable to react.

"How bad is it?" His mother is keeping herself strictly clinical.

"Look, rapid progression is fairly rare and, at the moment, it is not severe at all."

"What is it?" I ask.

"MS is an illness that affects the nerves in the brain and spinal cords," he recites patiently. That sounds fairly serious.

"Is there a cure?" I blurt out.

"Unfortunately, not yet."

I pause. "So it will just get worse?"

"Yes, that is the most likely turn of events."

His calm manner infuriates me: it is distant and impersonal, as if he has read all of the correct answers out of a text book and is ready to deliver them on cue but without any emotional attachment.

His mum is biting her lip. "What can we do?"

"For now I think it's best if we enrol him in some physiotherapy and…"

But I have stopped listening. I leap up and start toward the door, resting my hand briefly against his mum's shoulder before I leave.

He is sitting on the wall outside, head leaned back, eyes closed. I come up behind him and scrunch my fingers in his hair.

"Hey," I say lamely. He squints his eyes, looking up at me,

"Hey yourself." I sit with him and wrap my arms around him. "They told you then."

"MS," I say.

"Still want to marry me?"

"What?"

"I heard you say that you were Mrs Cultz," he teases.

"Yeah, well I wasn't thinking." That's the truth; it had been an instinctual response.

"True." His voice is hard now. "If you thought about it, I doubt you would."

I glare at him. "How dare you presume what I would want!"

"Woah, I've just been diagnosed with a critical illness and you're yelling at me? Really?"

"It's not critical," I say, "we're going to be fine."

I sit back to look at him and he is staring out at nothing in particular. His face is working hard against showing something.

"What?" I ask slowly.

He draws in a breath tightly then shakes his head.

"I'm not allowed to drive anymore."

Then, without warning, he begins to cry. I have never seen him cry before. For a second I don't know what to do, but then I put my arms around him and hold him and gently stroke his back, just as he did for me when I told him about my dad. We stay like that for a long time. He has his head leant against me until his mum comes out, holding files of information and tablets for the symptoms.

When we are huddled in the backseat together, I am struck by an idea and I'm suddenly back to my practical self.

"It's quite simple," I tell him. "I'll drive and you'll navigate."

I think it is the first time I've done something for another person because I want to, but I truly do. I can't bear to see all that potential go to waste and for him to miss out on the things he loves in life. He is someone who deserves happiness, someone that you can't quite believe exists because they are beautiful and talented and funny and bursting with so much soul and spirit and vitality. They take life with a 'wait til you get a load of me' attitude and I refuse to believe that life would give him this in return when he gives so much. I know that this illness will not beat him.

***

I can't decide whether or not I believe in fate, but over the years of collecting there always seems to be recurring themes within people's life. It's as if 'fate' has made sure that, at some point, if they miss something the first time it happens, there are several more opportunities already in place to ensure they stay on course. Hmm, I'm going to miss being able to muse over my theories. I love this job; I love the freedom to access millions of thoughts and make their thinkers' lives important. Alas, this will not be a privilege of mine much longer. I am almost done. My place will be passed on and I have been allowed this final collection of stories. So let us return to it, and to the character I may have inadvertently made the protagonist because I feel it will suit the reader and, quite simply, because I like her story.

Over summer the young girl went for a lot of walks by herself. She still felt lonely and trapped but these were feelings so familiar to her that she no longer fought them.

SABINA: 2.7 minutes

I long to ring Mona or Molly but know I won't hear from them until school starts again. I spend as much time out of the house as possible and I avoid my stepfather at all costs. I think about how in olden days they used to use leeches to suck out illness from people, and I wonder absently how many leeches it would take to suck all the evil out of Clemence. This leads me to imagine him covered in blood-sucking leeches and I smile.

I reach out my arm and run my fingers through the corn which is not yet ripe. I like walking by the farmers' fields and glimpsing the animals. I walk near the edge of the hay field and I can see the tractor in the distance. I scuttle to the hay bales and clamber on top of them so I can see down into the piglets' pen. I watch them transfixed for a while, mostly because I can't believe something so pink and soft and adorable will grow into something so huge and bristly. I have decided that pigs undergo the worst transformation of all animals.

Then I play for a while in the hay bales, pretending the ground is lava and making daring jumps to safety. Suddenly I hear the tractor stop. It is nearer than I realized and then the swearing starts. I freeze, thinking I've been caught. I'm scared that he'll shoot me for trespassing, as I know farmers carry rifles on them. After a while I poke my head around the hay bale cautiously, hoping he'll listen to my pleas before he pulls the trigger. But the farmer is staring at something on the ground and rubbing his forehead, then swearing again. Then he sighs and slowly raises the rifle I knew he'd have. I climb on top of the hay bale to see what's down there and, staring into the barrel of the gun, is an injured deer. He pulls the trigger. I scream as the creature's head implodes and blood splatters the golden hay around it.

Am I constantly going to be surrounded by dying animals? Can't I request a different recurring theme in my life? How about love? I'd rather a cliché then these repeated morbid occurrences. I am shaking and sobbing, curling in on myself. The farmer looks distressed.

"You weren't supposed to be here. What are you doing here?" he asks gruffly but I ignore him. He goes on. "They like to nest in the hay this time of year and sometimes I don't see 'em. I ran over this one's legs. I had to shoot it or it would have died painfully. Don't know what to do about the baby though.'"

I open my eyes, and huddled into the hay, shaking just like me, is a baby dear. His eyes open and meet mine; he has tiny white speckles across his head and down his back and there is a little of his mother's blood caught in his fur. I instantly recognize a fellow loner, a fellow survivor. The farmer sees me eyeing him.

"You could take him. He'll die out here alone. You'd be rescuing him, you know. You'd be a hero." I nod, drying my eyes.

He picks up the deer, who is probably still in shock because he doesn't move, and hands him to me.

I cradle him he whole way home, stroking his head gently. Then I sit with him by a small puddle and gently clean his fur. He whimpers and snuggles into me, breathing in my scent. I shrug out of my cardigan and wrap it round him, hoping that it will help him dry off. I decide that I must name him as this will officially make me his mother so I study him and then come up with Nenny. I'm worried that as soon as he finds the strength to walk, he will run away, so I hurry back to the house and curl up on the sofa with him.

When I wake up he is still in my arms, which I find enchanting, like I am at one with the wild. I bring him water in a bowl and, not knowing what deer eat, grate some carrots and bring these over to him too. At first he is shy, trying to hide in the gap in the couch but I understand. After all, he just saw his mother get shot this morning. Then slowly he takes the food off my hand and his tongue is rough and tickly, which makes me giggle. I watch him then stroke his head and whisper, "We are the same you and I... You're Nenny and I'm Sabina."

CLEMENCE: 3.4 minutes

I don't bother knocking anymore whenever I pass Hildi's house. I just walk in. Today I hear the shower going and I quickly strip off and join her. I hide behind the curtain then whip it back, making her scream. It's quite fun to watch that moment of terror as she stands, defenceless and naked, but she quickly relaxes and wraps herself around me. I'm due for a meeting at the main office later that day so I don't have that much time. I press her hard against the shower wall and begin.

Once I am duly satisfied, I dry off quickly and leave, knowing that I will just make it in time. I grab ten franks she left on the dresser and use it to pay for a cab.

I am introduced to the head of the typewriter firm who is surprisingly warm to me and takes me out to lunch.

"Mark had a good eye when he hired you," he chokes out between shovel loads of steak, "best figures I've ever seen, by a long chalk"

The man seems to talk almost entirely in clichés. Oh God, that's something my mother would notice.

"My point is," he continues, "you really are a bit of a diamond in the rough and I think you and I both know, as intelligent men, that you're wasted in this door to door nonsense!"

"What would you suggest I do instead?"

"Well, my dear boy, myself and the other forerunners of the company were mulling over figures and worked out how much income would increase if everyone on our selling team brought in figures as high as you." He took a gluttonous gulp of wine which stained his top lip off-puttingly as he continued. "We want you to devise a program teaching people how to sell and then run it for all of the various groups we own." He spreads his arms wide as if expecting me to leap into them or something. "What's the matter?" he booms. "Cat got your tongue?" He laughs.

I am intrigued by the offer. "Would my salary be different?" I ask slowly, "because, being honest with you, I am struggling financially."

"Ah yes, yes, I knew you'd be a details man. Makes for good business, eh, get down to the nitty gritty straight away." I smile trying to be patient. "Now, only time will tell if it works, but if figures increase for the company dramatically then so will your salary." He winks. "We'd like to start running the programs in three weeks. Do you think you could have a sales course perfected by then?"

I nod, my mind already beginning to fire off ideas.

"Very good." He pats my shoulder then orders more wine. "Now let's talk about golf!"

I tune out for most of the rest of the conversation, simply uttering "yes" or interjecting a laugh to keep him content. My mind is already working in overdrive and I am driven by this new purpose, determined to prove I can be a success.

ANGELICA: 4 minutes

I can't see Jack as much as I'd like to during the exam period, but he jokes that now at least he'll have an excuse if he fails as memory problems are one of the many symptoms. I know he won't fail though; Jack's smart, almost as smart as me.

As soon as my last exam is finished (I try not to dwell on how difficult the final question was) I hurry over to where I'm supposed to meet Jack. We said we'd catch a movie and then go back to his. We watch the new adaptation of *A Streetcar Named Desire* and although I find it a little dull, Jack is transfixed.

"You liked Blanche Dubois?" I ask him.

"No, it's not about liking the characters, none of them are likeable, but that doesn't mean it wasn't brilliant."

"You have to like them to be entertained by them!"

"I disagree with that. I don't think a good film is for enjoyment."

"So why would you watch it then?"

"It's an experience, it makes you think... I don't know, just the writing... some of the lines. What did she say? 'I don't want realism. I want magic! Yes, yes, magic!' Come on, you've gotta admit that's kinda wonderful?"

I'm laughing now. "Yes, when you say it I'm more convinced then when some dumb blonde is prancing about saying it."

"I don't know how you hated it so much."

"I think she reminded me of my mother."

We cross the street and loosely link arms whilst walking across the park.

"Take your shoes off" he says.

"Why?"

"I want us to feel the grass between our toes."

"No, come on, let's just get home," I protest, but he pulls me to the ground and removes my shoes.

"No, come on," I repeat.

"Uh, lets live a little!"

"No," I say more quietly. "I promised your mum I wouldn't let you do anything stupid." He sits back on his haunches and looks at me. "You know, the whole thing, you're more susceptible to... stuff. I don't want you to catch cold or something..."

"I'm not dead yet." He grins then tears at the grass a little. "We said this wouldn't change stuff with us, I don't want you treating me like a patient." I shake my head. "So, you either come run barefoot with me and feel alive or…"

"I never could argue with you!" I interrupt, picking my shoes up and grabbing his hand.

We walk with our feet against the wet grass without any barriers and it is peaceful. He smiles at me, enjoying the victory, and I roll my eyes.

"Tomorrow we race?" I say.

He nods, "Tomorrow we win."

"Look, I don't know if that's realistic with me driving…"

He turns to me dramatically and recites, "I don't want realism. I want magic! Yes, yes, magic!" and I laugh and join in with the second part of the line while my fingers play with his hair.

"Also, I've got an interview next week with a law firm," I say. "I wondered if you would like to escort me?"

"I'll check my schedule, I'm pretty busy an' all, but I could maybe squeeze you in."

I smile. I know he's not allowed to work at the moment and so he pretty much spends all his time helping me.

We take the train to the law firm and I have to help him with the ticket barrier because of the tremors and I pretend that this doesn't bother me. He keeps his hands along with his ticket in his pockets.

I search hurriedly for something to say.

"Sorry we didn't win with me driving," I start, and we spend the rest of the journey with Jack giving me tips on rally driving. I enjoy listening to people who really know what they are talking about.

I am offered a paid internship at the firm, shadowing one of the divorce lawyers with a view to becoming full time after that, depending on my results.

"You know one of the amazing things about you?" Jack mused, "I don't think I've ever seen you get nervous for anything. You just don't."

I shrug. "These things are always anticlimactic."

"It's kind of impressive."

I raise my eyebrows enjoying being called this and thinking that it suits.

We get herbal teas from a bourgeois café in town. While he is ordering I notice an old paper which covered the crash and I quickly find a bin and shove it in. We sit in the corner on plush seats and I automatically give him my pack of sugar too because I know he likes his tea sweet. I stare at him stirring his drink and I am suddenly bombarded with euphoria. I think that's the word for it. I feel filled with something good that he is here, so filled with potential, and I am hit anew with desire for him.

"If you could do anything in the world, what would you do?" I ask.

He leans back in his chair, shrugging his jacket off.

"Hmm," he takes a sip of his drink, "I'd probably say, 'Darling let's be adventurous, and pack our bags and just walk off in to the world.' Escape and explore."

I lean forward. "Where would we go?"

He chuckles. "We would kayak through purple canyons and stand on deserted snowy peaks and eat white strawberries and sleep on warm rocks beneath the stars. Be fearless."

I nod, knowing we will probably never complete this wish.

"That's your ideal?"

"No, I mean ideal would be red strawberries but you can't have everything right?"

He grins at me and I undo my hair from its tight knot and shake it out, relaxing into the afternoon. We decide to hire a bike. I steer and stand on the front forks while he sits and pedals, holding on to my waist. We cycle to a circular weir with a bridge over it and park the bike, lying down on the bridge with our legs dangling off the side, the gushing water surrounding us. With my head leant back across the stone, I can feel the vibrations that run through it as well and I let it rattle my body slightly, imagining what it must be like to not be able to control it.

"I got something for you," he says, touching my hand gently.

I sit up intrigued and he pulls a chain from his pocket and gently fastens it around my neck. I run my hands along it and I can tell it was expensive. At the end of it hangs a delicate ring, with a beautiful emerald woven into the mold. I study it, transfixed by the beauty.

"I didn't trust myself to get it on your finger."

He laughs, and I meet his eyes.

"Wait is this... a... proposal?"

He nods, running his hands along the ground studiously.

"I wasn't going to, I wasn't sure you'd... want to." He looks up at me clutching the ring. "But then I thought, sod it, why shouldn't I have a chance to marry the woman I love?"

I leap onto him, holding him against me. I'm sobbing idiotically, probably spoiling my carefully applied makeup but I don't care. I kiss his cheeks, his nose his hair, his lips and then we are laughing.

"So is that a 'yes' then?"

"Of course. You know I'm yours forever."

He pulls me against him and gently brushes his lips across my forehead and I can feel him grinning. He pulls out a second chain and hands it to me and I know it has the man's equivalent of my ring hanging on it. I reach up and fasten it around his neck.

"I love you," he says, and I know that it is true.

MANGOS: 5.6 minutes

It was a lavish wedding and I had a ravishing bride. Despite her refined appearance, there is something intrinsically interesting with Lou, something unexpected.

There were several society parties surrounding the wedding which we promised to have in England before we left, and I noticed that sometimes she could talk for hours, amusing and captivating the entire room, yet at other times she would lose the urge to speak entirely. She could also listen intently and nod solemnly while her mother ranted on about how I smoked like a chimney, and then bend doubled over with unrestricted laughter if I whispered a dirty joke in her ear.

For the wedding itself I insisted that all my friends travelling with the opera attend, which livened up the event considerably as with us came our old Greek traditions. Lou seemed to adapt immediately to the circle dancing and plate smashing, all of which made her beam with excitement. I liked how my friends marvelled at her and I felt sort of proud too, like I had discovered something others may have overlooked; like I was a key that had unlocked this hidden attitude within her.

The cake was excellent as well, with rich icing, and much to the distaste of most of the British guests, we scooped large slices into each other's mouths once we'd cut it. Lou insisted I sing instead of doing a traditional 'first dance' and I stared straight at her the entire time. Although she was red as sunset, her eyes glistened with appreciation.

SABINA: 2.6 minutes

Nenny has grown little horns which he loves to chase me around the lounge with, in an odd version of 'it', except I genuinely play not to get caught as his horns are actually quite painful and can now leave a mark. He loves the game.

My parents are aware of him and I am allowed to keep him on the strict condition that he does not sleep inside. One night, when there is a storm and lightning keeps dancing threateningly across the sky, I beg them to let him sleep on my bed but they are unrelenting. I stubbornly grab my duvet and Nenny and I walk over to my tree house where I set up a nest for the two of us. I lift him in and we both snuggle under the duvet, the wooden roof keeping the rain off and our combined body heat keeping us just warm enough. I whisper him stories of the Famous Five and Sherlock Holmes that I practically have memorized to soothe him through the storm and I seem to find a kind of solace in the embrace of unhappiness because it is more familiar.

ANGELICA: 4.4 minutes

We are walking, as we often do, along the beach, the wind whipping my hair aggravatingly across my face.

Eventually he tucks it down the back of my shirt so that he can see my face fully. We talk of the wedding. I think we should have it next year so we can plan properly, as I don't have much time with my new job, but Jack wants it sooner.

I notice him slowing his pace then he stops. I frown as he seems slightly breathless. I know he gets tired more easily these days but we've only been walking for about twenty minutes.

"Do your legs hurt?" I ask,

"No," he lies and unwillingly sits on the sand as if his legs have just given up. I sit too.

"It's the breeze," I say. "I'm finding it tricky to breathe too."

This is a lie but it seems to offer him a bit of comfort.

"I'm just acting up so that you'll take pity on me and give me what I want," he laughs.

"Well, that's just stooping too low, and you know it won't work."

"I know... you're the most stubborn person I've ever met.'"

"God, how romantic!"

"Don't you know that tactic? Insults as a form of seduction?"

I grin, glad for his quick quips and easy teasing. I follow his gaze staring longingly at the waves rolling toward us and I know he wants to run into their embrace, but neither of us mention what we would have once done unthinkingly because it is not a good idea when he's so susceptible to other illnesses. I've been reading through the never-ending lists of symptoms so I know what to look out for.

"I know," I say suddenly. "Let's go for a drive round one of the tracks, see if we can beat our last time."

He grins, feeling impulsive too, and I help him up, taking a shortcut back to the car knowing that he is tired. We stop at a red light having been chatting about which car we should use at the track. I check my mirrors then turn right.

"Angie.'" There is a shocked intake of breath. "We have to go home"

I glance over at him and he is covering his face with his hand.

"Sure, we can be there in five minutes," I say, taking the next left instead of a right. "What's the matter?"

There is silence. "Jack?"

He still has his face covered but very tightly, with no inflection, he says, "I've shit myself."

I can hear that he is on the verge of breaking down and know that I must keep it together, that I must not be repulsed, that I must remember that this is Jack. I knew this could be a side effect.

"Ok," I breathe, "don't worry... let's open the windows and we'll be home soon.'"

I try to pretend that the smell doesn't bother me while wanting to scream and be sick, but I am strict with my nerves.

"Oh God," he moans, "I'm so humiliated."

I'm humiliated for him. I want to make a joke but I can't; he is the one with the jokes. Besides, this isn't funny, it's pitiful.

"It's not your fault," I tell him.

"I'm sorry," he chokes, and I can hear that he is struggling to breathe through tears and he is shaking again. "I know this is difficult because of your father too... I ..."

He bangs his head against the window, as if he can make himself disappear or make himself wake up from a nightmare. And I let him because I don't know what I can do.

I park outside his house and get out the car as calmly as possible and slowly breathe in the fresh air while walking round to his side. I undo his seat belt and help him out. His mum comes running out and we both get him inside and peel his jeans off, throwing them into a bin bag. Jack looks tortured and horrified and the stench is overwhelming. I run a bath for him and his mum gets him in. It is hard to look at someone you love in the same way after you have witnessed something as degrading as that, but I kiss him on the forehead and shut the bathroom door, letting him soak as if everything is fine.

I go downstairs to freshen myself up and his mum is doing the same.

"Thank you," She says.

She smiles and I shake my head, unsure how to respond. "No problem" would be a lie and I'm too shaken to talk anyway. She gives me a hug and finds me a change of clothes.

I hear her knock on the bathroom door, checking on Jack. He's barely even allowed an unsupervised bath these days. I catch a bit of what they're saying. His mum laughs and jokes, "Well, at least you know she really loves you. I'd say that that's pretty much the ultimate test."

I don't hear him join the laughter but I imagine that it would at least make him smile.

A bit later I knock on the door, knowing that his mum helped him out of the bath a few minutes ago. He has a towel wrapped around his waist and is perched on the edge of the emptying bath. He looks better.

"You ok?" I start.

"Are you?" He shakes his head. "I'm so sorry."

I wave my arm vaguely, dismissing this, and snuggle into his warmth. He still has a way of radiating heat.

"Water under the bridge," I say smiling, knowing this will remind him of his proposal and I feel his body relax a little. He strokes my hair absently.

"You know, this has made me think… realistically we should do this wedding sooner rather than later."

I try to lighten the conversation by joking, "But I don't want realism, I want magic!"

"What?" he asks worriedly.

"It's a joke… you know, that line you liked when we saw *Streetcar*?"

"Oh right," he agrees absently, and I'm fairly sure he can't recall it,

"We'll talk later," I say and kiss his head gently and shut the door behind me.

My heart is full and I slide down the door and feel myself start to cry and silently mouth, "Where's Jack?"

CLEMENCE: 4.1 minutes

I have just completed my first training program and I am tweaking it back in my hotel room, which the business is paying for, when the phone goes. No one ever calls me; I have no one. I let it ring and go back to writing about personality types and then there's a knock at the door. Reluctantly I roll of the bed and answer it.

"Telephone for you, sir."

I can't believe someone has actually walked all the way up to my room to make sure I pick up the phone. I roll my eyes.

"Thanks," I say sarcastically, and when the phone goes again I get it, just so that I can be left in peace.

"Clemence?"

"The one and only."

"It's me."

"Hildi?"

"Yeah." Her voice is muffled and high pitch,

"What do you want?" I ask, thinking that she's probably noticed some of her cash missing and is going to threaten me.

"I don't really want to do it over the phone."

I laugh. "Sweetheart, we'll do it as soon as I'm back in town," I say seductively.

"I'm pregnant," she says slowly. I say nothing. "It's yours."

Everything looks like it's in slow motion and I feel nauseous. The impulse to break the phone over the bed passes through me briefly but then fades and I just feel drained.

"Are you still there?" There is a loaded silence which I know, as it grows, is my escape route passing me by.

"I'll see you when I'm back," I say and hang up.

***

I'm trying to decide which memory to present to you next and which makes most sense in the overall story. That's a lie. I know what must come next but I'm stalling... I don't want to relive this. The illness memories are particularly painful to Angelica and so I will convey them as briefly and factually as possible.

She wakes up at 5.20 a.m. every morning and goes to the salon to get her hair and makeup perfected before work. As one of the very few women in the industry, it is important to give off a good impression. She then picks up Jack, who now needs a wheelchair as he is not particularly strong and his lower back muscles cannot function properly. They buy their train tickets, and then they chat on the train, just as they had that first time. Some days it is almost like old times and the wheelchair is the only sign of illness, but other days are terrible. She wheels him through the town and into the court with her, then parks his chair at the back as he likes to watch her work.

She is famous all over Munich for her determination, not just as a woman in a male-focused business but the local papers repeatedly covered the devotion Jack and Angelica display on a daily basis, as if they are celebrities. People go wild for the tragedy of a rally car driver who could have made it but was held back by illness, but still manages to hold onto the love of his life. They make it glamorous when it truly is not.

SABINA: 2.9 minutes

I decide to sign up for the school ski trip this year as last time I went skiing with my family, it was a bit of a disaster. Molly signs up too and we promise to share a room together.

A week before we are due to leave, however, Molly catches flu and is forbidden to go and kept in the quarantine section of sick bay. I find the teacher in charge of the trip and tell her that if Molly can't go, I don't want to go either because it's not fair on Molly. She snaps at me not to be ridiculous and hits me once on the back of my shoulder with a ruler for being ungrateful for the opportunity as well. I run down the hall on the verge of tears, overflowing with indignation, and in a slightly frenzied state of mind. Everyone is constantly telling me I am ungrateful. I want to do something to prove them wrong, to make them see that I am actually independent; that I can take my fate in my own hands that I have a right to chose where I go and what I do!

Somehow I have found my way down into the cold kitchen and I am holding some frozen peas against my stinging shoulder when an idea hits me. When on cleaning duty once, I had decided to organize the bottles according to label, and there were four of them which had a strict warning of DO NOT DRINK across them. I quickly find one that fits this criteria. It's bleach. I'm assuming that it will make me ill and then they can't make me go skiing without Molly and that will serve them right.

I pour an ample helping into the lid and, for a dramatic moment, I feel the urge to recite that bit before Juliet takes the potion. Then I down it and begin to gag as my throat constricts around it, rejecting it. I begin to retch on all fours and I suddenly gripped with a fear that I may have killed myself. This is instantly accompanied by a triumphant feeling of how guilty all the grown-ups who have made me unhappy will feel.

I wake up in the sick bay feeling much better. I can see Molly's bed from where I am through a glass panel and she is staring at me anxiously. I smile, knowing we must have both missed the ski trip and she shakes her head in disbelief then mouths "Thank you"' I curl up around my aching stomach and sleep some more.

I'm woken by the matron's cold hands on my head and I stare blearily up at her.

"Ridiculous thing to do," she is muttering, "she'll be fine now though."

I look over to see who she is talking to and see my step-dad hunched there.

"You're lucky to be alive." She continues fussing over me. I don't feel particularly lucky to be alive with him glaring at me. "Your father's here to take you home so you can recover fully."

And although I protest, he drags me kicking and screaming to the car. I know he's been drinking and that I will have to fear for my life the entire way home; every time we turn a corner you can hear the empty bottles thrown in the back rolling and hitting each other jarringly. Apart from that it is a silent car ride.

As soon as I'm back, I go for a walk and call for Nenny. I'd let him out in the wild before I'd gone back to school that year and he had gotten big, his horns now grand antlers. He still always came running when I called and I hug his neck. He looks strong so he's clearly finding enough food and he walks behind me a while, sometimes even gently nudging my back with his antlers like he used to.

I don't know where my mum is, probably working somewhere, but it doesn't worry me. I spend my evening reading in the silent house. In the morning, after a walk with Nenny, I search for Clemence, already desperate to be driven back to school, but he doesn't answer my calls. I eventually find him in the attic, in an old armchair, cradling a large empty bottle of vodka and staring eerily ahead. I can barely make my way towards him, the floor is so compact with empty bottles some of which are smashed. I freeze three meters away from him, suddenly knowing that he is dead. I'm stunned. I slowly wriggle the last empty bottle out of his grasp and sit in the corner, staring at him, and it occurs to me that despite its poetic description, there is nothing noble about death, and the longer I stare at his motionless form, the more I want to live.

I try the phone but the batteries are still out of it so I have no way of contacting my mum. And so I am stuck in the house with a dead man until she chooses to return.

LOUISE: 3.5 minutes

I pat my bloated belly and rest my hands, as I so often do now, lightly on top of the bulge. The baby always loves it when you sing. It's also the only time I'm truly happy here, when we see your opera, despite having seen it at least fifteen times before. I clap and tear up all over again, as if for the first time. I know that you like me pregnant too, as I'm inclined to indulge myself more and my cravings fascinate you.

Despite all of this, despite literally being fused to another human life, I quite often feel isolated. My German is perfect and I don't talk with an accent, yet the people I pass still tend to stare at me as if I do not belong to this society. Perhaps it is all in my head, but it makes me uneasy in my own skin. Perhaps this is why I've grown fond of powdering my face extensively. It covers my blandness a little and also gives me something to do to look busy if I am caught in a large gathering with no one to talk to. It soothes my anxieties.

I've found that in conversations with people I don't know, I am overcome by this desperate urge to be liked and I am far too eager to please and overly smiley. I don't know what I am trying to compensate for. My job at the school teaching year four sometimes feels exhaustingly pointless too and the staff room is always filled with worrying theories that a war is coming. About the only time I have peace is when I sink into this red velvet chair, and know that for the evening I will not have to think on anything, just be here with you, without talking, just watching and I relax.

ANGELICA: 4.6 minutes

He died with his train ticket in his pocket and his hand clasped tightly around his necklace. I know, because I was there.

We never did get married. "A lucky escape," my mother had mused, "or else you would have been a widower."

I throw myself into my work and I am ruthless with winning my cases. My exterior is always perfectly put together. I am calm and determined, while inside I wilt. I was lonely so it is unsurprising that I said "Yes" to going out with Hannis when he asked, which didn't half lead to gossip: "Moving on very quickly," "Well, it must have been hard being tied to him for so long." None of these things are said to my face, I suppose my stony glare warns people away.

Through it all I hold on to what Jack once said he'd believed; that armed with a soul you can survive death, and no one had more soul than him.

It is summer and the heat is unbearable, I have to force my long hair into a tight plait to keep it off the back of my neck so I can work. The heat makes those I work with drowsy, which ruffles me and I snap meanly at a young trainee who is complaining of having to wear a tie in this weather. I inform him that standing in heels with sweaty feet for eight hours and maintaining a full face of makeup is not a breeze either, and that he is going to need more staying power than that if he expects to be employed.

Hannis insists I need to get out. What I actually want to do on my afternoon off is lock myself in my room, turn on the air-conditioning full blast and sit at my dresser facing the large mirror and just be left alone. I am well aware that this sounds vain though, and I had promised Hannis a date, so I go. He has tried very hard. The whole affair is almost too thought out, like he hired scouts for the perfect location.

We cycle up to this secluded cave where it is cool and thick brush hangs over the opening. Our voices echo and you can hear the soothing trickle of water and I know that this is a very romantic location, according to the book. What men never seem to grasp is that romance doesn't work unless the woman loves you, so when she doesn't it is clichéd, hollow and meaningless. It's like when you taste a shop-bought pie as opposed to a homemade one; it appears to be the same but it is just a little too sweet and there is something vaguely plastic about it.

Hannis walks around the cave, telling me stories of how some people think it's haunted and I force a laugh for his efforts. He clowns and pretends to fall off the edge and all I can think is it would be more amusing if he did, but I keep smiling and try to put a lock down on my snide thoughts that I can't seem to control. He sits next to me on the cool rock and leans in. I know what his intention is and I feel that I don't really have a choice but to kiss him. He, almost slyly I think, has trapped me in a cave and if I refused him now, we would have to cycle back down together with that issue and I don't have the energy for it. So I kiss him back.

Walking back to where we parked the bikes, he won't let go of my hand and keeps bringing it to his lips and planting a kiss on it. I force my smiles and squeeze his hand just because it is the only thing I'm holding on to. Although he is the one causing the discomfort, I need to let it out on someone and he's the only person there. He keeps talking of what we will do tonight and all I can think of is how quickly I can be back at the bottom of the hill and get away from this.

I cycle ahead and let the wheels roll down the hill, hardly braking, until it occurs to me that if I fell I would be stuck here with him so I exercise a little more caution. I thank him politely and promise him a second date. Then I practically run home trying not to cry the entire way.

SABINA: 3.0 minutes

In the summer term we are now allowed to look after pets and me and Molly help Mona with the rabbit her parents gave her. I have named the bunny Mumelmunch and he is rather lovely with floppy ears and black velvety fur with a white splodge over one eye that, in my opinion, gives him an edge.

We sit on the lawn in between classes and put our legs together, making a run for Mumelmunch, while we chat and bask in the sunshine. Sometimes the newspaper boy will jog along the road near us with his bulldog and wolf whistle at us, just to wind us up. Molly looks quite flattered but Mona always has something clever to yell back, which keeps him from coming over.

Today Mona holds up Mumelmunch's front paws and makes him do an excellent cover of 'Ride a White Swan'. Mumelmumch is completely oblivious to his talents and that makes it more entertaining. After the paper boy's normal greeting, Molly blushes stupidly and I tut dramatically at her.

"You don't want someone like him anyway, Mol," Mona states, as if she is an authority on the topic.

"I don't remember asking you guys to make my romantic decisions for me."

There is a pause and all three of us know that the knickers incident is hanging in everyone's minds. We never really talked about it, and it was a long time ago now, but suddenly she laughs and then I go too and we are all hit by a bout of that unshakable, contagious, can't-breathe-anymore kind of laugh. Mumelmunch looks at the three of us in concern.

"If you want to discuss boys," Mona starts, "I probably should let you know that I now have a boyfriend."

This is news and we both stare at her.

"Why didn't you tell us?" Molly squeals,

"Well, I just met him over the holidays. He's lovely. My parents hired him to clean our pool and his name is Johnny.'"

"Oh, that's a good name!" is Molly's answer and I frown. Is there such a thing? And if there is, then how would she know? Which names qualify?

But Mona looks chuffed.

"What kind of stuff do you do together?" I ask,

"Well…" Mona raises her eyebrows.

"Apart from that kind of stuff?"

"We mostly swim in the pool together."

"Oh, that's really romantic," Molly croons.

"Yeah, but what do you talk about?" I persist.

"I don't know, mostly the pool and stuff."

"It sounds wonderful," Molly says, scratching Mumelmunch's ear.

I frown, less convinced.

Mona nudges me and says, "Don't get jealous, Squirt."

"I'm not!" I protest. "I think we have to meet him before we can call him 'wonderful'."

I'm not sure if I actually am jealous. I think about boys a lot and sometimes all I fantasize about is being in a relationship and being close with a boy in that way. I almost pine after it, yet at other times I can't think of anything more awkward or, quite frankly, repulsive about having someone's lips on mine. The idea makes me recoil and shudder and that makes me worry that something might be wrong with me. Surely the idea of a kiss should be appealing to all girls.

The bell interrupts my worrying and Molly scoops up Mumelmunch and places him back in his cage.

"He's not half getting fat," she comments, poking him. "Mona I think you feed him too much!"

"Bini's in charge of food."

I roll my eyes. "I feed him the right amount, I'm good with animals."

Maybe better than I am with people.

As it turns out, however, none of us are particularly observant as we are strikingly corrected on Mumelmunche's gender when we open the cage one morning and find a lot of black and white baby rabbits. My heart swells; I have often fretted that I might be incapable of love because of the lack of love I feel for my family, but that doubt is always shattered when I see baby animals. They are so much better than humans because you can love them on sight without the issue of personality getting in the way.

There is a slumbering fear with me, a sense of déjà vu, and I am extra vigilant around the babies for signs of danger in case I am a jinx. But he is dead. He cannot hurt me now.

The babies grow stronger by the day.

Mona has hired me and Molly to test her daily in the lead up to her communion on various sections in the Bible and on the answers to some religious questions. We reach one which begins, "What is hell to you?" I stare at her, waiting for a defining response, but she answers by the book explaining it as a punishment and where all the bad people end up in eternal flames. This brings to mind a painting I once saw of hell by someone-or-other Bosch but it really hadn't looked as simple as burning in flames forever. When I think of that hell, I wonder if Mona has grasped the concept entirely. I think on the painting and if I ever have to venture into hell, I know that the faces in the picture will be replaced by those of Miss Gesh and my step-father and probably also my mother and those boys who used to bully me.

I'm so lost in thought that I don't notice the paperboy's advance this morning until he whacks us both over the head with a rolled up newspaper, his growling, lumbering dog following behind. Mona snatches it out of his hand and, in retaliation, he snatches up one of the baby rabbits and runs off with it. Molly is the fastest and doesn't miss a beat in chasing him and me and Mona try to cut him off by running from either side, but he seems to enjoy the attention of the chase and only stops when Molly starts screaming unstoppably.

We run over to see what the matter is and she is staring down at seven headless baby rabbits; the foul dog still has one body hanging out of its salivating lips and is chewing emphatically. The paper boy starts to laugh and croons, "Who's a clever boy?" at the dog, Molly is beside herself and Mona scoops up Mumelmunch, who is looking very distressed and little panicky squeaks are coming out of her.

I stare at the boy and all I can see is my step-father reincarnated right here, laughing at my inability to stop his evil. I grab the dog by the scruff of the neck and start dragging him away.

"What are you doing?" the boy yells after me, confused.

I hoist the useless mound of flesh over my shoulder; I am mere meters away from the compost heaps round the side of school, and also mere meters away from the incinerator. He realizes what I am going to do just seconds too late as he sprints manically toward me. I lift the lid and drop the dog into the fuming depths, shutting the lid forcefully. The boy is ready to jump in there after him and Mona and Molly have to restrain him.

"Why did you do that? You're crazy! You're going to hell!"

They hoist him away, saying, "It's too deep. You can't get him out without killing yourself."

I can see that the boy wants to throttle me.

"My dad's going to kill me!" he cries.

But I storm past him. "Sorry I can't deal with this right now," I say, "I have funerals to attend to."

CLEMENCE: 4.4 minutes

I marry Hildi because I'm not sure what else I can do that isn't abominably cowardly but a part of me believes this was her intention all along and, although I don't say it, I resent her for it. I feel like a dog in a cage a lot of the time when I'm home; the woman does not interest me, I do not like children and yet, somehow, I am a husband and a father. Perhaps its karma. I must do penance for my years of sin, but I don't really buy into that.

And I suppose having a family to support couldn't have come at a better time. I have developed my own training programs and they are selling like wildfire, and now many major companies are interested. Somehow I have locked into a new craze and my programs are regarded as somewhat revolutionary. It is by focusing on and expanding this that I remain sane. I sober up, knowing that this is a higher calling and the money begins to match my prospects and creativity.

Hildi thinks I am brilliant, but then anyone who knew their times tables would be considered a genius in her simple mind. I am reaching, and almost superseding, my aim of respected business man. The things I have been convinced for so long that I am destined for are finally falling into place and it helps to humor my family more if I imagine that a stable-looking life gives me more respect in the business world.

My years of observation have paid off and my principles are fairly simple, though I am cagey about them with people I don't trust.

1.I start by shadowing a member of the company, observing what the average person does and how they are instructed. Based on this and the company's aims I can establish what needs to be worked on.

2. I develop a personality profile which all attendants must complete. This way we can see where they work best and what needs to be worked on within each individual member.

3. I teach this concept to them so that they can appeal to their desired markets or audiences more cleverly and effectively by working on an individual's strengths and weaknesses.

4. I rework the communication between company members, different levels of the company and the company and the outside world.

Despite my growing success, I have reverted back to taking extensive night-time walks across the city. I always bring a notepad in case I get an idea. Here I do not have to be my usual extroverted cameo role that I have grown to play in everyday life.

I leave the house most nights, unable to stand the sound of my sleeping family. It is terrible that they can annoy me even in sleep. My son's features resemble Theo's and I simply can't like him and look into his face at the same time, though for a while I honestly did try. Similarly with my wife. The only time I like her is during sex, because probably it is her only calling in life, the only time she is actually passionately engaged or involved with anything. As soon as it ends I see her as her vapid self once more and I feel empty. Each sleeping breath they take now aggravates me more until I am driven from the house. I am thinking of buying a new house, something far more extravagant then Hildi's place, but I am going to wait until I am truly secure and then I will sit back and soak up my wealth and I will love it.

After a training session in Berlin, on my way home I pass a frail mother and child hiding, huddled in a rug behind some bins. I have heard of the escapees crossing the Berlin wall and some instinctual part of me takes an instant liking to them. I respect people who try to escape their destinies, who are brave. They deny all of this, of course, but when I offer to buy them food in return for their story, the mother is less defiant. I take them to a fast food joint because neither of them has ever seen a hamburger in their lives and they relish it.

The kid goes through handfuls of French fries, grinning from ear to ear and trying to chew all at the same time. I am oddly humbled when they start at my offer to get them desserts as well and then ask me what a banana is. I try to explain it, and then order a banana split for them instead.

I have no idea where this day came from. Perhaps it was a blip in the grand plan and it was supposed to belong to someone else, but all the same I give them some start-up money and the address of the Berlin branch of the typewriter company and tell her to say I sent her and she needs a job. Then I meander home, rather happy with my day.

HANNIS: 4.2 minutes

At weekends I always take Angie down to the boathouse. Sometimes the sailing parties are on and other times we have the place all to ourselves. I had already cleaned it up for Rita when she gave it to me and I now think it looks quite respectable. I open two beers and take her up to the small bedroom with the window that overlooks the lake. Rita had caught us today before we got down here, wanting to meet her and giving me an approving wink before we left.

The sun is hitting one side of Angie's face, casting the rest into darkness, and her long dark hair is plaited and runs in line with her spine. I reach out and run my hand along it, loving that I can do that. She turns to me suddenly and I wait, hesitant of what she will say. We have never talked of Jack together and I do not want too. How could I properly comfort her when, in all honesty, his death has been one of the most wonderful things in my life. Not the fact that he died obviously, but the fact that I have her because he is gone.

My hands are on either side of her and she is leant back against the door frame, I begin to kiss her, ignoring her initial reluctance. She pauses and looks at me, then begins to talk slowly and I can see it is difficult for her, as if she is trying to reveal a little piece of her soul, but the words are funny and I can't seem to form the expression she wants, something about how erotic it would be to be surrounded by ambulances. I begin to laugh. She walks away and scoops up her beer, sitting on the bed, taking large gulps.

"What are you talking about?" I ask, still laughing but also slightly worried,

"It doesn't matter," she replies flippantly. But I sense that she is no longer in the mood for closeness so I sit on the opposite bed, quite a tactful move I think. I will wait until she is ready. I've waited my whole life for her I can wait a little longer. I try a few jokes to try and cheer her up and then resort to distraction.

I know the boathouse has old windsurfers and I suggest this, motivated by the fact that she will have to be in a wet suit. I sit on the edge of the jetty giving her directions as I already know how to windsurf and she does not. She gets annoyed and flustered after dropping the sail for the umpteenth time but once I demonstrate the balance, she gets the hang of it more and floats gently back and forth in front of me.

"Where are you going?" she yells, when I get up,

"To get a camera, you're a sight not to be missed!"

***

I watch his memory intently and am hit with a wave of annoyance that Angelica's memory of this time is not within her seven minutes as I would love to relive it from her point of view, hear her thoughts and feel her emotions. See how differently this colors something that for him was such an event. I watch him running back along the jetty and raising the lens and her gently floating toward him and posing obediently. He is utterly focused, as if taking a picture of a rare bird of paradise that might cease to humor him at any moment. To him this screamed romance, to her a favor.

LOUISE: 4.1 minutes

There is a lock down on all borders and we are not allowed to leave the country. I have not taken this well. Everyone believes that the outbreak of war is imminent and, if that is the case, then I want to be home, on my side, not stuck in enemy territory. What if I can never return home? It is predictable of me to liken myself to a literary hero in times of crisis, probably so I can pretend that I am of some importance or that my suffering matters, but the instant this happens I feel that I understood Dante's pain of being exiled. I spew these thoughts out in a passion to my husband when I get home. I can see that he is worried too; his ashtray is filled with stressed cigarette butts. However, he calms me by simply holding me and swaying, then he quotes the part I mean from memory. 'Del bello ovile ov'io dormi' agnello'... 'The cruelty that bars me from the fair sheepfold where I slept as a lamb.'

"I feel the same way," he assures me, "but there is nothing to do. We keep a low profile, we continue to work, we continue to live."

He pats my stomach lightly and puts the Dante line to a ridiculous tune which is actually quite funny, and I soften, letting the tension trickle of me. I sigh as I feel it literally running off me before I realize that there is actually something running down my leg. I begin to scream and so he screams too, and then I laugh. He helps me to a chair and I know I'm about to give birth.

I'm panicking and he runs to call a doctor, "don't leave me alone." I'm yelling, "I don't know what to do!"

"Do you think I do?" he yells, while dialling the number.

"I don't know..." I'm babbling but words are always how I combat stressful situations, except with the pain distracting me I can't keep them in my head. "You know things, I'm always surprised by the things you know!"

"Yes well, I had a good teacher," he yells back, then he is talking to someone on the phone and I think I pass out.

All I remember of the birth is pain and someone shoving a flannel in my mouth, presumably to stop me talking so much or screaming. I don't recall which. When I come round I am hit by nature's absurdity; how could any human being instinctively love something that has caused it that much agony. This all changes the moment Stefanos hands me our child , the only words I can find to capture the wonder of what I am holding is that he is literally God's Gift and Stefanos, on hearing this, suggests we call him just that. And he is christened, Theodore.

SABINA: 3.3 minutes

The school gave us an option to spend our summer terms from now on working on a farm down south in the country and lodging with the farmer and his wife. The three of us sign up, joining a team of ten girls in total, eager to escape, and it is like I have finally found my home. We are woken before dawn and race down to the cow shed to collect the milk for breakfast. The first few mornings the race was out of eagerness but now it is to ensure that you don't end up having to milk Buttercup, who is the fattest cow ever and never stops moving. So, if you are the unlucky soul who has to contend with her, there will be an exasperating chase and you will end up covered in milk and smell for the rest of the day.

The couple are fairly strict but have simple values and are kind to us, and all of these are traits I grow to value. The farmer talks endlessly of the weather but not in the small talk sense; he is actually fascinated by it and very in tune with when it will change and how to read the signs. His teachings become fairly sacred to me.

The weather is a bit of an obsession of mine now; to look at the sky and be able to read the future there. To know from one look what everyone's mood would be that day and what duties we would do. It is like being given secret glasses that decode the sky and, whenever I am on the farm, I am looking up.

It is tough work, especially on days when you are put in charge of cleaning out shire horses. That's exhausting as their size reflects their mess. But I like watching my body change, muscles slowly being defined in my arms, and my skin becoming tougher and tanned. Freckles have emerged all over my face, which I hadn't noticed before, and I like to have these visual cues that make the change brought about by an experience more tangible.

The farmer seems to like me and one morning he holds me back, sending me up to the barn to help William rather than go with the others to lead the cows up to the field. He says with gruff sincerity that he sees me as very reliable and that I could be helpful with more difficult issues. When I get to the barn door, William is straddling a log and sharpening an axe. He is tanned and stubbly, rides a motor bike and always seems to be annoyed; I've heard him on several occasions refer to us as 'useless girls'. Although this riles me, I decide that being cordial to him will help the situation more.

"Morning," I chirp.

He glares up at me. "What are you doing up here?"

"Your dad sent me to help." He looks at me sceptically.

"Really? He thought you were capable enough for this?"

"Clearly," I say, glaring back.

"Did he tell you what we'd be doing?"

"No, but I'm sure I'll manage."

He nods, "Yeah well… we'll see."

He swings himself off the log, indicating that I should follow him into the barn. Inside there are rows of cages all of which contain chattering chickens.

"Here is our off-to-market section," he says pointing at the cages. "We gotta make a profit here so we sell our largest ones as meat. Today's the day they've gotta be killed and plucked."

I feel my jaw clench down; this is not how I want to spend my day.

"You need some guts to be able to do it." He eyes my small form. Despite being sixteen, I'm still fairly short. "So I'll demonstrate the first one. Don't wuss out, I'm gonna need your help."

He unlatches the first cage and there is a frantic flap of wings and doomed escape cries. He swiftly stokes down its wings and pulls it out.

"Now you're gonna have to hold it, cos this is kind of a two man job."

I replace his hands with mine and I can feel the chicken squirming against me as if it knows its fate. He swings the axe and makes a clean cut, but the squirming continues beneath me and I let go, disgustedly. The headless body begins to run around in circles and for a second I think that I am in a nightmare, that William will morph into Clemence and I'll be trapped in this barn with him and the axe.

"This sometimes happens," William says, calmly disposing of the head. "Their bodies can keep moving for quite a while."

I stare at it, repulsed and intrigued at the same time. He hands me the axe.

"Time to make yourself useful," he says, bringing the next one toward me and pointing to the place on its neck where I am to aim.

I raise the axe and he says to just pretend I'm chopping wood. My hesitation doesn't last long – after all I am no stranger to dead animals – and I help him with the rest without a fuss. I am sure he is mildly impressed. I don't tell the other girls, knowing they'd be disgusted.

That evening, when we have chicken for supper, there is a moment where I'm not sure I can eat it, but I feel

William's eyes on me from across the table and so I finish everything on my plate.

* * *

I snap the book shut, uncontrollable fear rushing through me. This is slowly replaced by confusion. I remember this. What I have just read is not fiction, that is how I first met my wife. I can remember her little determined face and my longing to be as fearless as she looked. What have I just read?

I go back and re-read it. I can feel myself panicking again. It's my name this person's used as well! They've changed her name, probably so I wouldn't know these events were real until I came to it. Then I relax. That's it. She didn't want me to know that she is the author. I cling to this strand of sense, unsure why she would not have told me she had written a book based on her life. Does this mean the other characters involved were all real people?

Intrigued, I continue reading.

* * *

ANGELICA: 4.9 minutes

All throughout summer we must attend these wretched boat parties because Hannis seems to be the star of the show and me his showgirl. This is a role that I am not well suited too and I have come to the conclusion that I am far better at being impressive then intimate. That is to say, that from a distance I seem like someone you would be desperate to know, but actually I am not easy to talk to. Hannis, of course, makes up for my avoiding trivial conversation by doing enough talking for the both of us and we visit every little group of people at these events and entertain them. He knows each of them by name and his affection does not seem forced. It is as if he genuinely wants to care for all these people. This is not a trait that warms my heart, though. In my opinion, love is only real when it is exclusive and Hannis loves everybody.

His friend Rita, who looks as if she's ready to drop off at any minute and isn't helping this fact by downing the alcohol, is just as much of a socialite as him. The two together are unbearable. At every party they have the same repertoire; the topics of conversation barely vary and I want to tell them all to actually think rather than merely talk. I know my thoughts are harsh but at least I'm honest, which is more than anyone here can say.

Mercifully Rita is too sick to join the celebrations today so I am standing with Hannis under one of the large new boats he has just won a race in, and a group of cackling woman surround us. It is one of those overused jokes which he tells because of their guaranteed success rate. Jokes are his social weapons and this one is utilized in boating situations. This is a concept I dislike to begin with; to live your life by tried and tested scripts with insured results.

"Woah!" he whistles obtusely as we saunter over to the group of woman. "She is beautiful... look at the legs on her!" Then he lowers his voice, "What I couldn't do with these."

The first time I was introduced to this particular gem, he had explained to me, when I hadn't laughed, that the two prongs at the back of the boat which the propellers are connected to are called legs. I don't laugh at jokes that are funny because a man is objectifying something as he would a woman, but all the girls at the boating club are besotted, throwing back their heads to allow room for their dense laughter. I watch pudgy Anna Maria's cheeks, which have doubled in size to accommodate her grin, and the strain seems to be showing as her dimples are deepening, threatening to cave her entire cheeks in.

"Are you ok?" he asks, pushing me uncomfortably against him. "You just don't seem like you're having fun."

"No, it's all been very entertaining," I sigh.

He laughs. "I know you're difficult to please, but this will definitely entertain you."

He leaps over the bar after this and nudges the unsuspecting barman out the way. Then he proceeds to flip bottles and catch them in the other hand while pouring drinks and putting on a proud show for the delighted crowd. He is loving it, his face the image of self-absorbed smugness. The way I imagine God must have looked when he finished creating the world: look what I can do, I bet you can't match this. He pops an umbrella in the drinks then picks up a piece of ice and flips it up his arm then flicks it into the drink, but after three success, he misses one. The ice skids along the floor and his mood changes so suddenly that it makes me laugh hysterically. He picks it up and makes some quip about 'You win some you lose some' and no one else cares, but I can't stop laughing. He hands out the drinks and wanders back over to me.

"You're right," I say, "that was entertaining." But this sets me off again and, although he looks hurt, I can't stop.

We mingle some more but his heart is no longer in it. I can see his intense disappointment with himself, which is ridiculous because all that happened was he dropped a piece of ice, but to him it seems he has failed being at being 'the can do' man.

"Are you ok?" I ask innocently. "It doesn't seem like you're having fun anymore?"

He sulks for the rest of the afternoon, disappearing off to see how Rita is. I actually have a nice time. I get myself a gin and tonic and sunbathe on the wall behind the boathouse where it is quieter. Gently I run my fingers over the necklace I always wear and wonder what Jack would think of the person I am now – the person I've become without him.

SABINA: 3.5 minutes

I like to keep myself busy, and so while everyone else has a long break for lunch, I ask the farmer if there are any other tasks I can do. He tells me that I could walk Kleiny and also tells me that William will show me where he is.

I go in search of William and hear loud music blaring from one of the rooms I see the W on the door and knock, assuming it is his, but he clearly can't hear me because of the music. I listen closer and realize that I know the song, 'Children of the Revolution'! I burst in about to yell, 'I love this song' but I am caught off guard because William is dancing manically to the track, arms and legs everywhere, his eyes shut and his lips mouthing along to the words. I have an urge to dance too but he's opened his eyes and run over to stop the music, instantly back to his more sullen expression. He is clearly embarrassed and is mumbling something and stroking the back of his head and when I ask, he quickly chucks me the lead and hurries me out.

Kleiny's name turns out to be ironic. The dog comes up to my shoulders and licks my face excitedly when I strap the collar on. I do not walk him because I cannot walk him: he walks me. In fact, this is an understatement as, for a large portion of the way, I am actually on my stomach, being bumped along the ground as if I'm a cart driver who has forgotten their cart. It is painful and fun and the only time I get a rest is when we come to a pond and Kleiny leaps uncontrollably in. I collapse and let him paddle about contently so I can catch my breath.

After a while, my attention is caught by the way the light dances on water. Light and water, both equally difficult to chase or catch, are the perfect dance partners. My philosophizing can't last long when I am smothered by a wet dog, though, and I am dragged all the way back. The aptly named Kleiny refuses to stop and pulls me round the entire farm, much to the amusement of the farmer and his son. They are in fits of laughter by the time Kleiny decides to end the walk.

* * *

I can hear Sarah at the door and I hover, unsure whether to hide the book or admit that I have read a fair deal and that I sort of love that she has written a book that includes our lives. I drop the book behind the radio and turn it on. By coincidence a Marc Bolan track is being played. She drops her bag on the floor and grins.

'Oh, this song!' She runs over and grabs my hand and waist, beginning to dance me round the room. The girls run in behind her and join in. 'This was one of my favorite songs when I was your age,' she says to Phoebe, who is fascinated by this, and instantly states that it is now one of her favorites too.

As the song comes to a close and we all strike grandiose finishing positions, I turn to Sarah.

"If you weren't in the training business," I ask, "what would you want to do?"

She does a double take. "Well, that's irrelevant cos I think I'm pretty stuck there now."

I put the kettle on. "What about being a writer?" I say.

"What's made you say that?"

I want to tell her that I've read it, that I'm touched by it, that I feel like I've fallen in love with her over again by fully knowing her young self.

"I feel like there is a lot to write about in your life."

"I tell you what would be wonderful," she says. "To write one book that makes a lot of money and then never have to work again." She pulls me closer. "Just think about it, all that time we'd have together!"

The wonder gently fades from her eyes and she takes a sip of tea. "How was the interview?"

"Bizarre," I say and we both get a good laugh out of the day's strange events

* * *

LOUISE: 4.6 minutes

Wartime is brutal. It seems as though life is cheap and with this knowledge, its value also decreases. During my second pregnancy I was sure that God would grant us a girl and I had decided on the name Clemence for her, which comes down to meaning 'mercy'. When it transpired that in fact we were getting another son, I had already grown rather attached to the name and, admittedly, the expected gender. In those young years I am sure it does not matter particularly to the child how you choose to dress them.

The war really began to take its toll around Clemence's 5th birthday. As our own small protest, I only talk to our children in English and Stefanos talks to them in Greek. This keeps us clearly divided from the world outside as language can be one of the greatest barriers; our different choice of how we address the children also seems to have put a slight barrier between us but I let that go.

ANGELICA: 5 minutes

It was inevitable that he would propose and how else but to make it a showy affair: a big announcement on a makeshift stage at a boating party. Predictable. The cheers rise up as he slips the ring on my finger, with everyone ogling at us, but I feel nothing. He says nothing privately to me once he has sealed the deal with a kiss. The first person he talks to is Rita, who is wrapped up in blankets but clapping enthusiastically. She kisses him proudly on both cheeks and whispers something to him that makes him laugh.

We move into his mother's house with the promise that he will buy us something wonderful when he starts making money. When that will be is unclear but he is too proud to use my savings. His mother recommends some papermill job, which he reluctantly takes.

His mother is a drained-looking woman with whom I do not get on particularly well. My main comfort at this time is that I can keep my old ring without anyone thinking it's odd.

SABINA: 3.6 minutes

My first thoughts when I wake up now are a day is a day, and it's not to be wasted. With that I can easily get myself up. I walk Kleiny once a day and often Will comes along too and we talk about T-Rex albums. I tell him about my parents and he doesn't judge me, he just listens. After a while I think we must be together because he waits for me for lunch and stuff like that, and I like that he does it, but we don't really comment on it. It's sort of just normal but it fills me up with a good feeling and so I hold on to this. For three weeks, for the first time in my life, I feel important and then I notice a subtle change. Will is slightly less confident around me and doesn't let me handle tools as much.

I seek Molly out and ask for her advice and she hurries me into the kitchen and shuts the door.

"I didn't think he'd believe her," she says, hurriedly.

"Believe what?" I ask.

Molly goes back to kneading dough too intently and I can see her gnawing on the inside of her cheek, like she always does when she's nervous.

"Mona cornered him the other day and I overheard her talking about you..."

"What did she say?"

"Well, she was asking him what you'd told her about your family and he was pretty cagey. And then she sort of convinced him that you were sort of delusional..."

"Delusional?"

She nods, "and that you actually killed your stepdad. But you make up that other story and believe it because you feel so bad." I stare at her. "I think she's jealous, and you know how she gets."

I have gone very still. "That was a horrible thing for her to say," I announce slowly, trying to control myself.

I don't know why this affects me so much, but it's probably because I wanted my step-dad to die and I feel guilty for that. William probably thinks this is why I was so good at killing the chickens – because I'm a psychopath!

* * *

I stop for a second. "Who was that girl you were a bridesmaid for years back?" I call out to Sarah.

"Who?" she asks, poking her head around the door,

"The girl you were friends with as a child, who got married to that guy from India?"

"Oh, God, Mona!" She laughs. "I once put a cowpat in her bed as revenge for… God knows what, but we were always playing pranks in those days.'"

"Yeah, I know,"

"Of course, she was there when we met."

I nod. Her work phone goes off in the other room and she rolls her eyes with a groan and leaves to get it.

* * *

I storm out of the kitchen and up onto the cow hill. The light is just beginning to fade. I know exactly what I'm looking for but I have to be selective. The right kind of cowpat has to be crunchy on the outside but break open to the smelly mess within under pressure. One that is simply runny or crispy will not work. I find the perfect one and gently slide it onto a towel; it is large and full of promise. I think there is a sense of poetic justice to me using her own formula against her. 'After all,' she had once told me, 'people are at their most vulnerable when they're in bed. And everything is twice as bad because it is their little sanctuary, their place of rest. Destroy that and you got 'em; you got 'em good!'

I slide the cowpat very gently under her pillow.

We all get ready for bed in the bathroom and I run into my bed and curl up, filled with evil anticipation and try to look like I'm asleep. However, trying to sleep feeling so on edge would be like a mouse trying to fall asleep in a cat's ear. Mona is one of the last in the room and I hear her fall back on her bed just as the farmer's wife clicks off the light.

For a while nothing happens and a few people drift off but I know that it has cracked open when she lay back on it. A slight smell drifts over to me and I hear her shuffling confusedly in her bed. I hear the pillow turn and a head settle back into it then stop moving suddenly. Then the squelch of a hand investigating under the pillow. And then a scream. Someone clicks the light on and I look straight over at the screamer. Mona's pillow, face and hand are covered and she is prancing about enraged while everyone else tries to dodge whatever flies off of her. The scene is excellent and the success of the payback warms me. 'I got you good,' I think to myself, admiring my handiwork which is still running around the room.

Some of the older girls tell her to shut up and sort herself out and let the rest of us sleep and they click the light off again, yelling at her for the smell. In the darkness I hear her having to strip her bed and clean herself off without anyone's pity, and it serves her right.

In our last week on the farm, Will asks me to meet him in the garage, saying he has a gift for me. When I get there, he is leaning on his little blue motorbike and grinning.

"I've saved up for a new one," he says, "and I want you to have my old one, a sort of 'to remember me by thing' and also as a way to escape your house when you need to."

It is the most thoughtful present I have ever been given and I am touched. I feel myself welling up. "For God's sake, don't cry about it," he smiles and then he kisses me lightly. I like it. "Also, I know you didn't kill your step-dad... and I heard about the cowpat." He raises one eyebrow.

"Now that I will plead guilty to," I admit, and he shakes his head, chuckling, and I join in.

MANGOS: the 7th minute

Perhaps there is only ever one way you are supposed to die, and no matter if you run for all you're worth away from that fate, it will sneak up on you. This is the bitter irony of me having lung cancer. Thinking I had escaped my destiny of my lungs giving out on me when I ran away from sponge diving all those years ago was clearly too simple an escape. It turns out it's been growing in me for years; a time bomb that has finally made itself known. I only went for check-ups when my singing became affected, and now singing even simple tunes grates the inside of me and falls flat on other people's ears.

It is a harsh truth you will eventually grow to despise even the things you love. The pain makes me bitter, which is something I have never been, and my wife's various antics are less charming to me than they once were. I am put out by her pretence that Clemence is a girl and I talk less and less, which is unbecoming to me as words and song have long been my passion. Theo asks me why I don't read to him anymore. Me and Lou used to curl up next to him and read him Dante and Shakespeare, determined at first to do parenting right – to educate and make our children cultured.

With my voice rapidly fading, however, it is unlikely that I will ever have a proper conversation with Clemence, let alone help to shape the man he will become. The opera company had to 'regretfully' let me go and money is now tight. That, combined with war rations, combined with pain, is enough to almost change the essence of who I am.

I heard someone once say that the only good thing about old age is respect, but how can I be respected without my voice. My status as a talented singer feels like it has been stolen from me and my jolly outlook shrivels up with each new burst of pain. I try hard to stay true to myself, advice I have lived by and influenced others with for many years, but sometimes when we are all huddled in an air raid shelter and the ground trembles, I pray that the next one will hit us and annihilate us all.

HANNIS: 4.5 minutes

I am surprised my mum suggested this job. We both know how my father got in with the company – an elaborate affair with the woman who owns it – and now the pair of them are ridiculously wealthy and living an ideal somewhere.

The work in the lower ranks of the company is hard but I really work for the first time in my life, and although I feel a little guilty making money from a place that caused my mum such pain, I desperately want my wife to be happy. I will be the husband my father never was, I will make it work.

One crisp morning an official knocks on my door. I have a moment of fear that something bad has happened to my wife but it is actually someone here to inform me that Rita has died. I haven't seen her now for several years but the news still guts me. I'm overwhelmed with emotion can barely hold myself together.

"I know this must be hard for you," the lawyer says, "but I'm here to tell you that you are mentioned in the will. You probably know this?" I shake my head. "She has left you her property and her land."

I stare at him in shock.

"The house?" I say in disbelief.

"Indeed. Now, there are some legal documents you must sign if you are to become the rightful owner."

I take the rest of the afternoon off and think of the lovely Rita. I will be attending the funeral next week and I want to be involved in planning it. I think I know what she would have wanted.

We are going round to Angie's mum's house that evening. I've always gotten along very well with her and try not to let my recent loss affect the evening. Her mum fusses over me as always. 'What a catch!' she'll constantly stage-whisper to her daughter, and I can't understand why Angie doesn't enjoy these visits when her mother is so charming.

When we get to the dessert of homemade apple cake, which has the introduction of 'I think I'm finally taking to baking in my old age!' she begins to talk of how lonely the big old house is and how she feels she is finally ready to detach herself from all the memories it holds.

"Memories like me?" Angie asks.

"Don't be silly, Angie, you know what I mean."

"No, mother, I don't. Let's talk about this."

"It's so difficult to have a conversation with you!"

I decide to intervene and feel like it is a good time to break the news to them anyway.

"Well Ms Hammon, your timing for such a decision could not be better, for just today I have inherited a house. I don't know if you remember Rita? Well, it was hers, and I will be fixing up the main house for me and

Angie, of course, but you are very welcome to move into the boathouse if you want?"

She claps her hands excitedly. "Oh yes, it's rather quaint there, isn't it? Oh, don't you think it would be lovely, Angie?"

ANGELICA: 5.2 minutes

I'm in a white room with patronizing blue butterflies painted up the walls. The bastard that is responsible for this agony has not arrived yet but I am told that his message was "Try and wait until I get there" which only makes me scream more intensely. This feels all wrong. It should be your child, Jack. Why can't I have your child?

I felt like I was back at my final exams, staring at the last essay question. Come on, you can do this. One last push and it will all be over and you get that cloud-like headache that comes over your forehead and stops rational thinking. I scream again and the essay comes back into focus, except now the essay question is simple. With, perhaps an infinitely more complex answer. Do I want this child?

Hannis arrives once it is all over and is instantly in doting father mode, cooing and caring as if he knows it.

"I'm so sorry I'm late," he says gently, as if I'm an invalid, "but in all that time I had, I came up with a name." It seems fitting that he should name this child. His child. I feel disconnected from it already, as if it was never meant to be. He places her in my arms and she cries which is an unceremonious greeting and does nothing for my headache.

"Little Sabina," he says soothing her head, "don't cry, we're here."

CLEMENCE: 5.2 minutes

I have reached my first million. I am enthralled, overwhelmed and damn pleased with myself. I've worked bloody hard and now I'm ready to reap what I've sewn. I wish I knew my brother's address so I could send him an update. How he'd come grovelling. He'd finally respect who I am.

I love the respect that accompanies wealth and my name is becoming more recognized in elite circles. I'll go out to lunch with a potential client and a snooty waiter with a fake French accent will ask who the reservation is for. When I casually say it's for Mangos, his entire manner will change, he suddenly uses a lot of nervous hand gestures and laughs at anything I say. I always remain unfazed, pretending I have not noticed the change, but secretly I revel in it.

The one downside is trying to keep a reputation in check. No one has ever particularly cared what I did with myself before, but now there are standards to live up to; people are interested in how I live. Because of this I try to avoid having to take my family to important business events. To me they represent my life before success and they are remnants of a shady past that does not fit in well with this bright future. The only time I walked in to one of the business ventures with Hildi on my arm was a total disaster. It does not matter how much money you give the woman to buy fancy clothes, she can't help but look cheap. I can see some important men staring down her dress rather than at her face, meaning she does not have their respect, and on top of this her remarks are always twee and uninformed. Several times I feel my hand twitch and I have to breathe and count down from ten so I don't hit her.

I really shouldn't have to put up with this shit. I am successful, rich and attractive so why carry this burden of a woman who brings me shame. My whole life I have been chasing things I deserve and now I am getting them. This is not a time to settle, I am still looking for more. I resolve to divorce Hildi and when I tell her, she cries and hangs on me like baby baboon, with an expression just as stupid. Once I have batted away her frantic kisses, she tried to initiate sex, her only weapon, and truth be told I am sick of it from her and I slap her. Even she can understand that this is final and we set about looking for a divorce lawyer.

SABINA: 3.8 minutes

For our last year at school there is an extra-long ski trip organized and this time both me and Molly make it there. For the most part it is excellent and we are all shrouded in thoughtless excitement the majority of the time, the kind that would be annoying to witness if you're not actually feeling it. The headmaster (who gets the expenses for his family's trip covered by our parents and is supposed to be in charge of us all) disappears the minute we get there to enjoy the skiing and bars without having to look after a group of teenagers. Instead he leaves his twenty-something-year-old son in charge of us, who, in our opinion is arrogant and chauvinistic.

Not everyone holds this opinion though as I'm fairly sure by the end of the night he is in bed with one of the girls. We have been instructed to follow him down all the slopes and stick together. He seems incapable of doing this as he gets bored and won't wait for the slower girls. I know for a fact that for three of them it is only their second time skiing ever. Mona yells at him to slow down for them multiple times, but he doesn't care, and just to aggravate us and because he thinks it's funny, he leads us on to a black run. This is fine for most of us but after a few minutes a cry is heard and a ski comes whizzing past us. We follow the track it made back up to Judith, who is sprawled upside down in a painful position.

Molly and I begin side-stepping back up to her, while the headmaster's son laughs and skis off. I am outraged and yell abuse after him; he had a duty of care as the oldest and the one who was put in charge and he didn't fulfil it. I loathe people who don't come through when they've agreed to be responsible for something.

When we get to her she is practically hyperventilating and her legs are twisted at odd angles. We try to soothe her and stand her up but she screams ferally with pain.

Mona has now joined us, having retrieved the lost ski. . We end up making a ridiculous makeshift stretcher out of our jackets to get her down the hill and she screams the entire way until Mona shouts, "Shut up! You think we don't want to scream too? It's not like you're the lightest person to carry!"

We roll our eyes at her but it does quieten Judith to private self-pity which helps. We get her to the medical centre where it is revealed that both her legs are broken and I'm just about ready to strangle that idiot boy. The headmaster arrives with his son sometime later. He looks suitably abashed and I smile, knowing he must have got an earful from his dad. Our flights are rescheduled to tomorrow to get Judith home after casts are put on.

Feeling like a sort of hero does not last long. The first Monday after we get back, as I enter the school I know something is not right. The group of girls in the hallway seems to part as I walk through it and there are glares from all angles, including from people I have never even spoken to before. The classroom is also dead silent when I enter and before I can take a seat, I am stopped by Miss Gesh's cold voice.

"Don't bother, Miss Mangos, you are expelled."

I freeze, thinking this is probably a nightmare, and I try to look around for evidence of this.

"Yes, I'm talking to you, Sabina. The headmaster has taken that stint you pulled on the ski trip most personally. Endangering another student is unacceptable."

I stare at Miss Gesh in disbelief,

"What are you talking about? Me, Mona and Mol rescued Judith off the mountain after the headmaster's pig of a son so very irresponsibly…"

"I don't want to hear any more of your pathetic lies, Sabina, go and clear out your room."

I stand numbly, then, having no other choice, go back to the dorm. But I refuse to pack. I am not leaving a month before my final exams I have not sat through all of this to fail at the last hurdle. The exams are my ticket out, to a new life!

As soon as the bell for first break goes, Mona and Molly come charging into the room. I leap off the bed.

"What on earth is going on?"

They try and calm me but I can see that they're both furious.

"They lied," Mona states,

"Yeah, no kidding!"

Molly interrupts, "The story that the headmaster has told everyone is that his son was trying to keep charge but that you refused to listen and lead the four of us off on a black run when he wasn't looking."

"What?"

"He's protecting himself and his son. This way they are in the right."

"And he can get away with it cos... well, he's in charge. He announced it all this morning in assembly to everyone."

I clench my fists in rage. "Why me? Why not one of you?"

Mona bites her lip. "Probably because if he picks you, it's only you he's fighting... I mean your mum would probably side with them, she always has in the past."

I kick the cupboard and then begin to tip it over.

"What are you doing?" Molly shrieks.

"Grab the other end," I instruct.

I know that all the teachers will now be in the staff room enjoying their break and this is the only plan I can think of. We attract some attention as we drag the large cupboard through the halls and even some nervous laughter as we push it firmly up against the staff room door. I turn to the small crowd of students watching.

"Anyone who wants to seek a little justice for being wronged by a teacher, grab a desk and help us stack."

Within ten minutes there is practically a barricade preventing the door, the only exit to the staff room, from being opened. There is only a tiny window in the top right hand corner of the wall through which the smug chattering filters out. I take a defiant stance before our protest and wait.

Then come the bell, the realization, the confusion, the banging on the door, the protests of, 'What in God's name?' 'Let me try' 'Open this door, NOW.'

The cries become more frantic and our sports teacher's face pops up at the tiny window to survey the scene. Then it quickly disappears again with a look of shock and horror. There are more mumblings of, 'They've trapped us in.' 'What?' 'The students! The students have trapped us in.'

Laughter starts to erupt all over the hallway at the scene until a booming voice echoes, "Open this door NOW! THAT IS AN ORDER."

"Sorry, sir, I don't take orders as I have just found out that I don't actually belong here anymore."

"Sabina?"

The PE teacher's head pops briefly back up then hurriedly retreats again.

"Yes, it is, it's that Sabina girl."

"The girl's a psychopath!"

I sigh and grit my teeth and address the headmaster. "You are actually just the person I wanted to talk to, sir."

"It is this kind of behaviour that resulted in your..."

"Tell everyone the truth!" I bellow.

There is a second of silence.

"I have no idea what you…"

"Ah sir, let's not do that. Let's keep it simple. I will not open this door until you tell everyone the truth."

"I don't know what you are talking about."

"Well then, we're going to be here a long time."

There is an angry silence, then an eruption of banging from inside the room and it sounds like all hell is breaking lose. We take a seat and listen to them trying to organize, envisioning the scene. They try 'One, two, three push!' and then they try and find a phone. I think they even try to create a battering ram, but we were thorough and our work in impenetrable. The laughter and jeers only serve to infuriate our captives more.

We keep them there for four and a half hours before he finally cracks. His admission is pathetic and stroppy and I feel a victory cry rising up in me. I am Nelson! I am Fredrick! I am Napoleon! There are cheers as we unload the barricade. He has agreed to the conditions that I am no longer expelled and that his son will make a full apology to Judith. I figured the shame of everyone knowing he is a liar is enough on top of that and I saunter through the rest of the week feeling like the all-powerful server of justice.

ANGELICA: 5.5 minutes

Work is my only solace in this life and I am the best there is. I have just won the Pudarti divorce case for the husband to get custody of the children, which is highly unusual, but my passion is always deadly because I am thorough. I back up my arguments with fact and reason until there is nothing left to say and then I win.

My receptionist shows my next client into the office for the usual first meet and assessment. She is fairly young, a little too pudgy for my liking, and her shirt is too low. I take an instant dislike to her, but luckily for her I always separate my personal opinions from cases, because winning is all I care about. I tell her to help herself to biscuits and she goes through them like she hasn't eaten for weeks, which I know is not the case because she is paying me enough to feed a family of four for a month. She natters mindlessly away about being young and seduced, impregnated and how the husband wants nothing to do with the child but he is a millionaire and she wants a quarter of all his earnings.

"Seems fairly straightforward," I interject. "What about custody?"

"Oh, he doesn't want anything to do with Ben and he doesn't want to give us any of the money!"

She starts to cry and this exasperates me so I decide to use one of my little loopholes to cheer her up. It will also throw off the opposition, and he sounds like quite a powerful man, so this will help to shake him up.

"I tell you what Mrs Mangos, I have an idea." She looks up at me with puppy-like adoration. "I want you to take your husband's credit card this afternoon and go out and buy yourself whatever you feel you will need after the divorce – a place to live, food, clothes, school tuition for your son, whatever. Your husband will then be stuck with the bills because, according to my notes, he has agreed to be responsible for any debt on his credit card as of the day of the divorce. It won't have occurred to him that this will contain the charges made by his wife."

She looks puzzled but slowly understands and then giggles gleefully. "What else?"

"That's all you have to do for now, I'll sort out the rest. And be on time for court next week."

"Oh I will!" she leaps up and practically dances out of the room. "Thank you! I'm going to get Ben. We're going shopping."

I settle down to afternoon of case notes, research and as I begin to form an argument. I feel envious of this Hildi's silly little life; it must be wonderful to be so stupidly carefree, to not be constantly haunted by thoughts.

The first day in the court runs smoothly and the husband's lawyer approaches me at the end to try and make a bargain already. I pat his cheek pityingly.

"Too soon for that, you wouldn't want the opposition to think you were desperate, now would you?" and I sweep off to plan for tomorrow.

The only thing that was slightly off putting throughout the session was the way the husband rocked back in his chair contentedly, never lifting his gaze from me.

Before I leave my office that evening, I see a bouquet of red roses sitting at reception.

"A gentleman left these earlier, asking to see you. I said you were working and so he left them here."

I scoop them up and a note falls out, on which is written "Whenever I see roses I am struck by nature's ability to create perfection, and today when I saw these I thought of you. I hope they are being well cared for. Yours, Clemence Mangos, or from the side of the story you've heard, 'the bad guy'."

I have not been wooed for years and a part of me is charmed by such a bold act. I also want to laugh at the note and for a moment I think of sharing it with my secretary, but I don't. Instead I pocket it and take the flowers home with me.

* * *

That night I hear Sarah telling the story of her piano classes to Lisa who is giggling wildly.

"Daddy tells it well too!" she remarks.

Sarah sounds puzzled, "Does he?"

I smile to myself and walk into our bedroom. I sit on the bed, holding the book and deciding to come clean. I hold it up so it will be obvious when she walks in and she can just say, "So what do you think?" without me explaining.

She takes her time leaving the girls though and I absently flick through to where I was, not wanting to move from my chosen position. Something suddenly catches my eye — my name in bold at the bottom of the page. I have only been included through her memories so far and so this surprises and intrigues me. I glance over to see what 'I' have to say.

* * *

WILL: 4.4 minutes

"Can I help you?" a curt receptionist asks. She has a slight accent, French or Russian perhaps.

"Yes, I'm here for the interview," I state.

She smooths one side of her pristinely tied back hair and narrow her eyes. "There are no interviews today."

I stare at her, feeling embarrassed, though I haven't done anything wrong. "Sorry, I was under the impression..."

* * *

The book falls from my hands and I am motionless. That event happened just a few days ago, after I started reading the book and before my wife could have had any idea that it was going to happen, let alone write about it.

More to the point, there are still a lot more pages…

"What's that?" Sarah asks at the door.

An excellent question; what the hell am I reading? How does this person know about our lives in such detail? God, this makes everything real. These people – Louise and Clemence, I had known Angelica must be Sarah's mother– but they must all be just as real as me and Sarah. It's not stories I've been reading it's lives. "Just a book," I say a little numbly and hurriedly put it up on the shelf.

"Any good?"

"Yeh, it's fine." my thoughts are so disturbed that my words aren't coherent.

"I didn't know I'd told you about my boarding school stories," She laughs, "but apparently they go down well with the kids!"

"Uh huh."

"You ok?"

"Yeah, just tired," I say and roll over.

It must be some kind of practical joke. The interview must have been a practical joke, but to what end? Is this some kind of divine intervention?

I am suddenly struck by what I have been handed. I have been given a book of my life and the option of reading it. I stare at the book over on the shelf and I am thrilled and terrified. I forget the how and the why because I cannot start to answer those, and I need to take away the weight of their importance. The point is I have this, in my possession. Surely it can't be healthy to read on after this. What if I come across things I don't like in my future, or if I start to follow the events written like a script, or I get bored with what I know and live a sort of half-life?

But the people's lives I have come to follow… now that I know they lived, I have to know what happens to them.

Tentatively I pick up the book, as if afraid of what it might contain, and I scan the next few pages. There aren't any 'Will's on them. I wonder if I should avoid reading the 'Sabina's as well, in case I learn something of my wife's future, but I think if I exercise caution, I can just stop reading if I get to something that hasn't happened yet and it will be fine.

* * *

CLEMENCE: 5.8 minutes

I know that Hildi would never have had the brains to come up with a ploy like that so it must have been this woman. I am fascinated; what a sly move, a clever move. I watch her prowl between the jury and judge, effortlessly controlling everyone around her. She is everything a woman should be – beautiful, elegant, intelligent, powerful. I rock back on chair enjoying watching her and a powerful urge to claim her comes over me. I want her to be mine and I always get what I want. However, the perfect woman is something money can't buy. I imagine her on my arm at business ventures and it is a million miles away from the scene with Hildi; this woman has class. I imagine the way people will look at her, the impressed whisperings, the jealous glances and I want to drum the table with glee.

A few days after I send her roses, I receive a telephone call. The voice is low and pure. There is no hello, no formalities, she simply opens with, "I hope you understand the dangers of fraternizing with the enemy."

"Do you mean women?"

She laughs, "Yes we can be rather unforgiving, but don't worry. Mostly we take pity on the less intelligent gender."

"Mmm, that's an overgeneralization."

"Too true... I don't take pity on anyone."

I laugh. "Consider me warned. How are my roses?"

"I gave them to my husband as a gift."

"And does he take care of them properly?"

She sighs, "Yes."

I pause. "You see, things as delicate as roses need special attention, an expert touch. Anyone can think they're beautiful but not everyone can fully appreciate or understand them. Sometimes they need something more."

"Sometimes they do. What would you suggest?"

"Well, perhaps start with a luxurious evening out." I wait to see if she'll bite or if I have misread her interest.

"When?"

I already know where I want to take her. "There is a masquerade evening at the Château de Loir tomorrow. I'll pick you up at seven… don't tell your husband." I laugh again, "Or my wife."

I hear her chuckling darkly too.

"What sort of dress code is it?"

"I'll bring you something."

"I can dress myself," she snaps.

"Oh, I don't doubt it," I say smoothly, "but it will be more fun this way."

"Fine, if you're sure you can afford it, what with your credit card bills mounting up," she retorts, and then she is gone.

I chose an emerald green dress which hangs off her shoulders and down her back, and she is effortlessly stunning. We both hold our masks over our eyes and ignore all the loud socialites. We find a quiet table at the back, which is surrounded by circus performers who hang in the air from elegant drapes. It is obviously expensive, which I can see that she appreciates.

"Shall I get us Martinis?" she asks.

"Something non-alcoholic for me," I say, "I prefer to be alert when I'm enjoying myself."

I grin. I think this is the first time in my life that I am proud of the woman I'm trying to seduce but honestly, there is nothing I wouldn't do for that coy smile.

LOUISE: 5.2 minutes

Without the draw of his voice, the hold Stefanos had over me has faded a little and I frequently feel unfulfilled. This is probably why, when I am tapped on the shoulder by a British soldier and led into an alley way, I follow without hesitation rather than run away.

I have been recruited by the British government as I am one of the few Brits stuck in Germany who is fluent in German. They want to offer me the job of teaching British spies German. I am stunned and flattered into agreeing. I will be doing something important. I am given strict instructions, which send me into a panic already as I am not sure I can even follow them. I am not allowed to write anything down about them, in case their details are seen by my family or, worse, by someone inspecting the house.

The group lessons are so different from my memories of teaching the opera men. These boys are disciplined, attentive and professional. We talk of nothing else but the lessons and I do not even know their names. This means that before the lessons start, there is a patient silence where the gravitas of what I am doing can sink in sufficiently. At one location, me and one of the youngest soldiers were first to arrive. He was a thigh tapper, one of those men who cannot endure silence, and whenever it threatens they lose control over their own hands and cannot escape the rhythm. His taps were unmusical and reverberated eerily around the room. I probably remember this endearing little incident because the boy did not turn up to another session after that day, and although none of us spoke of it, we all mourned silently. It made me think of my two boys, my fear for them, and I want desperately to go home.

But I am not a child anymore and this defiance makes me strong, it makes me sound brave which is always something I've longed to be.

ANGELICA: 5.8 minutes

The thrill of an affair is a blessing. To talk and be entertained by someone's conversation rather than their clowning is wonderful, and to be seduced rather than molly-coddled is something long overdue.

The covert taking of quick phone calls while Hannis is in the bathroom gives us both a thrill as well. It is not just the secretive nature of our relationship though; I am very attracted to him. He is influential, successful and blunt. He doesn't say anything to save anyone's feelings so talking to the two of us together is undertaken at your own risk. My feelings toward him do not mean that I soften up on the case; nothing will interfere with my spotless record for wins and I actually enjoy arguing my point more with him smirking at me from behind the desk because we share this secret. And it is exhilarating to feign indignation. I even slam my hand down on his desk to emphasize a point I'm making, and our faces are inches away. I can see he wants to kiss me but I have to pull away and continue with the speech.

Today is probably the final day of the case, and as I talk, he pulls an apple out of his jacket pocket and makes a show of rubbing it clean on his jumper and then gradually twisting the stalk off. I'm watching him out of the corner of my eye. I begin to walk toward his table, still making my final case and trying to get his attention. And he slowly takes a bite of it, and then another, and just when I reach the corner of his desk, he puts it down angled toward me. The bite marks have left the shape of a heart. He is on the verge of laughter, mouth full of apple, and I turn away to hide my smile then conclude my speech, and win the case against him.

***

This whole thing is gnawing at me. Just holding the book makes me feel powerful. By the time I reach the end, light will have been shed on my entire life. I could know the best and worst moments of my life right now by flicking ahead through the pages, and I'm tempted. It is so tempting, which is odd because there are so many logical arguments against this but it is different when it is right there in your hand. I could find out whether I get that job or not, what my girls are like when they grow up, how I die... How my wife dies.

Oh God, I need to stop reading now. Why is someone doing this to me? I hold the book between my palms, rocking it back and forth. Maybe this is a gift, to be able to know what's in store for us all. Maybe this is the key to living a peaceful life, and if so, I can't just throw that away. I also need closure from these stories. Now that I know the people in them once actually lived it makes me care all the more; I can't abandon them mid story. So, hesitantly, I read on a few more paragraphs.

* * *

SABINA: 4.0 minutes

Two days after we finish school, I get a call from Mona at three o'clock in the morning. I can barely make out what she is saying. As soon as I understand what has happened, I take my motor bike make the hour-long trip to her house.

The scene is a mess. Her mother has shot her father and he is floating in the pool, surrounded by a cloud of red. It's strange how when you think a thought you've already had, it can instantly take you back to the first time you thought it. I am taken back to staring at my step-father's corpse and hit anew with how messy and unceremonious death is.

Mona can't bring herself to call the police, but at least she has taken the gun off her mother who is crying in the corner. I call the police for her and then help Mona drag her father's body out of the water and roll him over, but half of his face is missing and this sends Mona and her mother into fresh hysterics. I find a towel from the pool house and cover him up and wonder absently when I got so good at this.

When the police arrive, they arrest Mona's mother and take her father's body away. The whole thing is very dramatic and I'm fairly sure my friend has gone into shock, so I take her inside and just let her talk to me. Then I get her ready for bed and tuck her in, and she has to be coaxed like a child. As she sleeps I make the decision that I have had enough of this entire place and I resolve to find my real father in the morning, as if this will fill in some intrinsic gap within me. Mona and Molly are going off to university and eventually they will both be fine, but I still feel like there is something wanting.

I leave a note for Mona and I set off on my bike.

I find my father living in a wonderful house on a hill by a lake and it is only when I see the boathouse by the water's edge that I realize I had lived here years ago with Gran. And this confuses me. Then, the house on the hill had been empty and under construction. I still resent my mother for taking me away from my Gran when I was happy. I was allowed to visit her once in hospital before she died and she couldn't remember who I was.

He greets me warmly, and with relief, but you cannot dodge the fact that we are strangers. His wife is very beautiful with cropped blonde hair and she kisses me on both cheeks and tells me to stay as long as I like. It is clear they have a lot of money – apparently he inherited some kind of papermill – and is practically a millionaire. They talk of skiing in the mountains nearby at weekends and of sailing races that they do together.

We walk down to the boathouse together and a little girl in a swimsuit runs up to us.

"Daddy! Look, I can dive off the top step! Who are you?" she asks me.

"I'm Sabina," I say.

"Oh, hello."

She waves and then grabs my dad's hand and pulls him to the end of the jetty. He counts to three, then she bends her knees and dives off with a little squeal.

It is like I have unlocked the door to what might have been. I could have been this child – Katrin. I could have had all this, but and it is not jealousy I'm gripped with, but regret. I am realizing that it is too late to seek fatherly love. I'm nineteen now and I don't know these people, no matter how much I would have liked to.

The house has three levels and Hannis shows me to a room on the bottom floor. Katrin has grabbed my bag for me and is dragging it along the floor.

"Cool!" she says looking around. "I never come down here. My room's on the top floor with the best view in the house, right Dad?"

"That's right, kid." He pats her head.

"Hey, why's this picture of me in black and white?" she asks, picking up a photo stand from a table in the corner.

We both glance over and I recognize the picture; it's of me, when I was far younger. I look up at Hannis, wondering if he will lie or tell her who I am. He sits on the bed and, slightly reluctantly, tries to explain that I am her half-sister. The child looks up at me in wonder.

"You have to stay with us!" she exclaims. "I've always wanted a big sister! This is so exiting! Daddy, why did you never tell me? Why have we never met her before?"

He doesn't answer but scoops her over his shoulder.

"Time for bed," he says, swinging her round and she giggles delightedly.

I lie awake, not having found the solace I had hoped for. I don't know what I expected. He is happy and I suppose that is enough.

But I can't intrude on this happiness. I am not a part of it.

HANNIS: 4.7

I am utterly shocked when she says 'affair'. I hadn't ever suspected this, and it throws me into turmoil and makes every part of me ache. I was never going to be someone who got a divorce – I had vowed this to myself long ago. I had vowed this to my wife! I would make marriage work, but unbeknownst to me I was alone in this aim, and I can't believe this has happened. And that she was going to sneak out to leave before I got in from work. She didn't even write a note, I checked.

I am bewildered, in a haze. I grab Sabina. I have to get out of here, but I'm taking my child with me. I strap her into the back seat of the car.

"It's all right sweetheart, we're just going for a drive," I say.

I remember how scary it is as a child to watch your mum and dad fall apart. I hear Angie screaming from the balcony flat window and I shut the door to try and protect Sabina from this.

"Take your bloody stuff with you," she's yelling, throwing down my carefully-pressed work clothes, then harder objects like a suitcase. "Here's to the years of boredom." She's screaming manically.

I get in the car, shocked that she can be this cruel, this wild. I hear her running down the stairs.

"Oh, and you were bloody quick off the mark to swoop right in there after Jack died, weren't you! Don't think I didn't notice." I have no idea where this is coming from and I start the car in a bid to escape but she screams, "And if you think your taking my child away from me, you have to be insane!"

She is laughing and looks crazed. She rips Sabina out of the back seat.

"Careful!" I say as Sabina begins to cry, as if on cue.

"Get out the car, Hannis, We're leaving."

"Let's just cool off," I say. "We can move on from the affair, everyone makes mistakes." I move toward her, trying to soothe her.

But she pushes me away and lobs Sabina in to the passenger seat then starts the engine, shrieking, "Then Lord forgive me for marrying you!"

I am left watching her drive away with my child; with the life I thought we were building.

And somewhere within me, I felt that I knew this would happen. Like I had been treading on egg shells for years, trying not to displease the woman I loved. And now that my worst fear had happened, I am free. Somewhere ahead is a fresh start, a future with promise. She will be doomed by her looks, which will fade, but personality does not, and this is what I can cling too.

SABINA: 4.3 minutes

Unable to return to my mother, I use the remainder of my savings to move to England, the farthest away from her that I can afford to get. However, I fear that I will never quite be free of her neglect. I arrive with nothing but optimism and a dictionary. However, after a year and a half of cleaning toilets for a minimum wage, it is unsurprising that I was caught by her offer of working for the company on the promise that, when she retired, she would put me in charge and I would be secure for life.

I already know how to train people. I've had to watch her do it for years so I pass easily and I'm soon working among the elite of the company and, surprisingly, some of them are very bearable. I become particularly close with a man named Albert. I use the money to move into a shared house in Britain and fly over to do coaching sessions. This way my mother cannot tempt me into moving back in with her.

The first time Albert visits me in the UK, he decides it would be a good idea to surprise me. It turns out he was wrong.

I arrive home early because one of my best friends, Anne, rang me sobbing from the hairdressers, asking if I could pick her up. She had had a perm done and has also had parts of it dyed and she looks like a very unhappy poodle. I try to hurry her inside the front door before anyone can see her but she pulls me round the side of the house and whispers, "Bini, someone's robbing us!"

"What?" I peek my head around to the kitchen window and see the back of a tall man examining pictures and ornaments on the mantelpiece. I duck back down, panic spiking through my veins.

"What do we do?" Anne asks,

"Show him your new haircut," I suggest. "He'll run for miles!"

She hits me. "Bini, seriously! And it is too soon for hair jokes!"

I see that we are opposite the tool shed and an idea occurs to me. I get the shovel and sneak round to the side door.

"Be careful! He might have a gun," Anne helpfully adds.

I inhale, stalling for a second, and then burst through the door and knock the man over the head. He falls like a tree.

Anne hurries in behind me. "You got him?"

"Yeah, he's out"

"I'll call the police," she is saying as we roll him over. It's only when I see his face that I recognize him as Albert. He is groaning slightly; thank God I haven't killed him. I explain this to Anne and she finds the whole thing hilarious. When he comes round he is dazed and pissed off, but I tell him to be grateful I didn't chose the pitch fork instead. Eventually he sees the funny side.

On one of my work trips in Germany I bump into Will, whom I haven't seen since I was sixteen. I tell him that I still have the motorbike he gave me, not that it works anymore, but he seems chuffed. He asks me what I'm doing now and I explain that I'm hiding from my mother and he can't believe I work for her now.

"Get out of there! Run for the hills, I'm telling you," he insists, laughing.

It's strange but barely any time seems to have passed when we start talking and we end up at a makeshift carnival. I have to embarrassingly admit that I am terrified of rides so we just wonder round and catch up. He is looking to move to Britain too and I say that he is welcome to crash in our house until he gets himself settled. He takes me up on my offer.

***

Later that evening as she was wondering back to her hotel, she passed a hand-crafted bag stall that was set up a way out from all of the other carnival attractions. A beautiful bag with an elephant sewn into it caught her eye. If she bought it, the bag could remain a thing of beauty and purity in regards to the fact that an impulse of attraction to something, even an inanimate object and the subsequent freeing impulse of claiming such an object, creates a memory of a pure, happy moment. A perfect way to end the evening.

However, as she insisted on examining the technicalities and practicalities of the finely embroidered bag, she had found the zip too stiff and the stitching too loose, suggesting that the appealing bag would have disintegrated before too long.

I suppose this also holds true for life: everything can appear appealing, but when examined closer everyone's stitching is unravelling and your relationships, views, morals and family can fall to pieces as simply as an ill-crafted bag.

She thought on this and recalled her grandmother and Mona and Molly, and the other people that had faded out of her life. She realized she did not want Will to fade.

* * *

I feel an obligation to tell my wife what I have in my possession and ask her advice. But I also don't know where to start, how to explain the issue, and I don't want to distress her or burden her. I begin to panic. I stare over at her gently snoring form and know I won't wake her. I am alone with only the book and I know I won't sleep, so I admit defeat.

***

CLEMENCE: 6.4 minutes

I know that she will want something lavish, something to remember and which focuses on her, and I have the perfect idea. I have never been more convinced that I am finally on the right track and marriage to a respectable and impressive woman seems to encompass the next step in my success perfectly. I hire out the court for a day and pay actors to line the seats and even hire one to fulfil the role of judge, telling Angelica that Judge Benedict is absent due to illness and she begins her case. I hide myself near the back of the audience and, at the predicted moment, I stand and loudly and clearly state, 'I have an objection.'

Everyone freezes as she slowly turns toward my voice, looking puzzled. I walk slowly toward her, keeping her gaze locked with mine in the complete stillness, and then, once we are in the centre of all those frozen people, I get down on one knee and ask her. She is entirely caught off guard but I can see her eyes twinkling with pleasure at the display and she says "Yes". Although I expected this, I am slightly relieved; it takes a lot of self-confidence to organize a stunt such as this one. On cue the entire cast stands and burst into applause, including the judge, but I look only at her and she shakes her head in disbelief and admiration and I kiss her fiercely while the applause roars around us with equal ferocity. She wraps her arms around my neck and whispers, 'What was your objection?'

I lean in and, out of the corner of my mouth, reply, "My only objection was to your last name."

Although she hits me for using such a line, I can see that she is very pleased and, surprisingly, so am I.

WILL: 4.5 minutes

* * *

I pause as I read my own name again and decide I shouldn't read that section. My eyes automatically glimpse the first line and I throw the book across the room. I sit still, staring at it sprawled out on the floor, and wonder if I am descending into madness.

This is ridiculous. I should just destroy it and forget that it ever existed. I crawl over to it, noticing that it has landed on the same page, and I let my eyes skim over it to check for danger but I know these times very well. Mine and Sarah's (or Sabina as she is called here) wedding, so beautifully relived, that I get a bit emotional. I flick through the next few pages, knowing what happens, and pausing at certain highlights like the birth of our girls or buying the farm or the time where one of our cows escaped and we had to walk her back while holding up the M25 and making the morning news.

And I am again swayed toward the benefits of having such a book, a little memory bank. I stop flicking as I come across the next moment and read it in full, having never quite heard the full story.

* * *

SABINA 4.5 minutes

My mother takes everybody to the top floor, which is only used for parties and important clients, and there is a general farewell, congratulations, have-all-these-gifts feeling. Finally we are all sat down and she claps her hands together to thank us for all of our good work. She hopes that the next leader will bring just as much success for the company and that we will all work just as well for them as we have done for her.

I feel slightly electric – so much power, so many people working for me. I am finally going to inherit something of worth from my mother.

When she opens her arms widely and says the name 'Albert' I freeze. He gets up and bows his head in mock modesty and shakes her hand and hugs her and everyone claps. I refuse to make a scene but my body is coursing with anger. I have worked for her for years for practically nothing but this promise and I am done with her screwing up my life.

I stand up, snatch my coat up and get on a plane back to Britain, to Will and the girls vowing never to talk to her again. She is nothing to me now and this time I exclude her from my life. I will not come crawling back.

* * *

I didn't know that it was Albert who had been given the company instead. I am suddenly furious all over again. I want to know more and I continue reading.

* * *

ANGELICA: 6.1 minutes

To say that Clemence swept me of my feet would be an understatement. In such a whirlwind romance, it is easy to feel like your love is very special; like it elevates you above the common person the way a celebrity might feel of themselves.

I send Sabina away to live with her grandmother, checking first that Hannis is not living anywhere near the boats house. Apparently he's designing a house for the hill but does not live there yet. I promise myself I'll visit regularly. I want her to know and respect her mother, but a part of me also can't stand the child that forced my body to transform and who also belongs to a man I don't love. Honestly, it is far easier to think on her fondly when she is out of my sight.

When Clemence suggests that I give up my position as a lawyer so that he can train me in his business and then we can do the business trips together and be with each other more, I barely hesitate. I'm a fast learner and soon I am expanding on some of his original concepts. Within the first two years the company has grown into a tour de force and our programs are coveted. What follows are the blissful years. I am doted on by him, which adds to the feeling of importance and being cherished. I thrive under this kind of treatment.

We always book the penthouse suites of luxury hotel rooms when we do business trips and, neither one of us liking parties, we use the entire space for ourselves. We drink champagne in bubble baths and eat chocolates on ridiculously-sized beds. We share mean remarks and jokes about the people we have had to work with that day. We have compiled a strict judgment code and apply it to anyone ugly, unusual or stupid, the breed of people we cannot stand. For the first time in years, I am truly happy.

LOUISE: 6 minutes

I don't know if self-confidence is something that comes with age, or if it grows the more you do, but I have never been more self-assured. I am technically now a British spy and it is amazing how a title can cover over any personality faults you feel you may have. It's like they are erased by this answer. It does not matter if I'm shy or uninteresting or disappointed because I am a spy and this increases my value as a human being dramatically.

I finally feel like I deserve to be here. I truly believe that giving someone a higher cause is the answer to any of their current problem. Of course, I love my boys dearly, but I can see that life so far has been struggle. Theo no longer needs bedtime stories and exhausts me by traipsing round the house insisting we all speak German and prodding us repeatedly if he hears another language. Secretly I am worried that the Germans will get in to his mind and turn him into one of those child spies. Everyone hears the rumors, and I have overheard several gossiping mothers talking of the Samson case (whether it is fictional or not is unclear) but the parents were turned in to the Gestapo by their eight-year-old son for sympathizing with the Jews. At night I sit with Clemence in his room and shut the door so we can speak in English, which I know he prefers, just as I do, and this gives me such strong hope for the boy. Any child who can hold on to their identity whilst being surrounded by this surely must have strong morals. I look at the determination in his eyes and know that he will go far.

He once came home fuming about me having let him dress as a girl for the first years of his life, and I had to explain that I don't see clothes as defining you. He didn't speak to me for two weeks. I thought I'd lost him then; a sort of steeliness, a dangerous quality, had entered him as though he had lost some of his childhood. But tonight he is back to himself. I sit on the floor while he umms and arrs over which book I should read to him. We don't have many as I haven't been able to afford one since the outbreak of the war but I still have my original collection. He is smart and I really value this and he is quick to understand concepts when I explain them to him. He'll pepper me with endless questions about Shakespeare when I read it to him. We are halfway through *Macbeth* and he is fascinated with the idea of someone being able to do such horrible things to get what he wants.

"But why?" he asks again, looking up at me in astonishment.

"Well it's about ambition," I explain. "You remember we talked about ambition?"

His dark eyes meet mine widely as if his mind is opening out from within. I stoke his head gently and vow to myself that when he is old enough, I will tell him of my service in the war effort and he will know who his mother really was. He will know that I am strong. I convince myself that armed with this knowledge he too will want to be noble.

I never really knew what I wanted to be like, but I have stumbled into being exactly who I want to be, and this has blossomed out of the worst circumstance imaginable. Stefanos's magnetism was lost when he stopped singing and, although I still love him, it is more affectionate then romantic. I understand that now and I am content with it. I visit the hospital regularly and they tell me he has not got long left. I am compassionate and proud of his life but these last days do not reflect the person he was. He is broken and bitter and I have to imagine him on stage or at a party or arguing about books to cover up the evidence my eyes now give me.

* * *

The house is beginning to stir and I tuck the book under my pillow, as if I being associated with it is something shady. While everyone bustles around in the morning rush, I check my mail and have a notification from the company I interviewed at.

'Dear Mr. Tief, we are currently monitoring the position carefully and in all probability you will hear from us within the next few days as to whether or not you have received the position.'

I tap my hand agitatedly on the table. The thought occurs to me that I could know now. All it would take is a little skim reading. But I don't want to do that, so instead I go to the next section.

* * *

CLEMENCE: 5.7 minutes

There is only human gratification. Why deny yourself things? What is the purpose? What are you working towards? I seem to be able to get some sort of pleasure just from watching other people drink, like I'm an onlooker of my fantasy. Anything that can offer me relief in this moment is worth doing. I have tried not to drink and for a long time it worked. But I've God damn done it! I'm a fucking success! I've had a family, founded a company, proved I can do it all, so now I can do whatever I please.

I get up from the computer. I haven't had a drink for two days. I know she'll be listening out and I inwardly curse myself for hiding the bottle in the bread bin because it will make my retrieval more obvious. I slowly open the lid – I deserve it – and I find a glass. What good am I doing if I don't drink? Angelica has hidden all the glasses. I can't work without a fucking drink. I search for mugs instead, promising myself that I won't drink anything for the next week.

I give up on my search and gulp straight from the bottle. This is just a part of me. I shut my eyes and revel in the pleasure of it, then I begin to down it urgently before I can fully register that it isn't filling up the emptiness. I open my eyes and see Angelica's runt of a kid glaring at me. I hastily tuck the bottle under the sink.

"Just cleaning up," I say, but she shakes her head. "Don't tell your mum about this."

"I don't talk to my mum," she replies snottily and prances away.

I've got to do something about that kid.

LOUISE: 6.5 minutes

With the war over and Stefanos dead, there is nothing left to tie me to this place. I have been asked to return to Britain and been offered a position within the government. I cannot wait to return, for my parents to meet their two lovely grandsons, and to return home. For my children to see their true home. I tell Theo to find Clemence because I want to sit them both down and explain what I did in the war effort and to tell them why we should return. I am ecstatic. I feel like someone has unlocked the chrysalis and I can finally spread the wings that I have slowly been growing.

I have been trapped in grief and fear for so long that I am looking forward to a fresh start. I will always cherish Stefanos's memory and the wonder he gave me in regards to self-discovery, my sons, love and opportunity, but I am comforted that without him these things remain and I am still a whole person. I know his death affected the boys a great deal and I hope that we can build a successful new life when we get back to England and be happy, despite that.

I pack my favorite picture of Stefanos in my hand luggage because I couldn't bear it if something happened to it, and then I begin to hum his favorite opera tune to myself while I await the return of my boys and the start of our new life.

* * *

It's getting colder now and Sarah's brought in the logs I collected in and is making a fire in the lounge. Once it's going, she runs up to me waving her coal-covered fingers toward me, almost getting my face, then goes to clean herself up. I continue...

* * *

ANGELICA: 6.2 minutes

He is sitting opposite me at the kitchen table, his usual accessory of a generous glass of schnapps between his fingers. I don't know why he has told me; I would have never known. I know that he would have had no real feelings toward the girl he slept with. 'A drunken mistake,' he slurrily insisted. But I still feel violated. I do not like to be poked fun at. I do not like people taking advantage of me. I do not let it happen.

He stares at my stony expression and it is the first time I have ever seen him look worried. He clutches the glass more tightly and it breaks, but he doesn't flinch. His hand is bleeding as he says, 'Angelica I'm sorry.'

I nod and leave him to clear up the glass, knowing that we will go on for the sake of the business, but my one true thought is from something my father used to say: 'Drunkenness is never a defense in law.'

***

Her memories toward the end begin to blur but her last clear thought was in the form of a dream.

I'm in the dank cave and there is a massive stone slab in front of me and a lever in the corner. All at once the lever is pulled down by an invisible force and the slab rotates slowly, revealing two people frozen in a block of ice. They are always people I know and I must decide which one is allowed to live. Frozen in the ice is my daughter; she looks very beautiful and is smiling. Next to her is Jack, healthy and young. I begin to sob uncontrollably but I know I can't get out until I make the choice. I run my hands over both their frozen faces then step back. I have five seconds left or else they will both be lost to me forever.

I choose you, Jack, I always choose you.

***

It is frustrating to know that the story will have a definite end, that nothing more can ever be added, no matter how enchanted or frustrated I am by the person. They will remain crystallized in eternity as they are. I suppose the best comparison I can give you would be when you are in the middle of a wonderful book and suddenly it ends. You are left disconcerted and mourning the loss of the people you came to know, but they are unreachable through the barrier of the pages.

Such is my job. As it is not part of my job description to know how the person died, that is taken care of by others. Their death is, of course, not their memory and therefore I am not privy to this, so all my collections end abruptly without any closure for me. But perhaps this is a selfish view. After all, I am not meant to have views at all, merely observe, but everyone knows that subjectivity is impossible when it comes to human action. And so I hope you will forgive me for my own indulgence. Little did I know that this was not Angelica's end by far.

SABINA 5.6 minutes

I stand awkwardly at the end of the narrow pathway that leads up to the door, trying to somehow plan what I will say. I long to return home to the farm with Will, the girls are coming round at the weekend as well. But I had promised myself to finally resolve things with my mother. It has been over twenty years since I spoke to her. For a while she would send birthday cards to the girls, and sometimes even ones for me and Will, all of which I made sure were studiously ignored.

I have managed to find her address. I walk cautiously towards the door and it slowly swings open before I have reached it, which alarms me slightly. Assuming she saw me from the window, I hurry inside, but there is no one there. I drop my bag and look around. I can hear a faint, 'tick, tick, tick' sound.

"Mother?" I say quietly. I notice that she is far messier then she ever was when I lived with her, probably because she had me to clean. I catch myself; I have promised myself to keep bitterness at bay. The 'tick' sound grows louder and I suddenly sense a presence behind me. I spin around and there she is, standing on the stairs, staring straight at me, her arms outstretched. For one bizarre moment I think that she is going to run and embrace me. She looks eerily grand in a bright blue kimono that spreads out beneath her outstretched arms.

Then she opens her mouth and makes the strange 'tick, tick' sound that I have been hearing. The effect is very frightening and my first instinct is to run from the house, but a bustling young man emerges from somewhere.

"Who are you?" he inquires, quickly hurrying up the stairs and carrying Angelica down.

When I see her up close I am amazed at how old she is now and that she is not beautiful. Some old people are, but not her. Once I explain who I am, he instantly becomes unassuming and apologetic and explains that she had lost her mind several years ago. His explanation is interrupted by several outbursts of 'tick's. I am oddly moved by her current state and the knowledge that the wrongs will now never be righted. It also frightens me to death that someone of such gravitas, someone whom I so fiercely resented, has been reduced to this. I remember my grandmother not being able to remember me at the end and I wonder if this is hereditary. The thought makes me shake.

It is impossible to hate her now. I can barely decide if she is really human anymore.

"Sometimes she will recall things," he explains patiently. "Mumblings of race cars and the like, none of which make much sense."

"No, I don't suppose she knew anything about racing cars." I sigh. "Who pays for you to look after her?" I ask, knowing from my research that she had spent most of her savings in retirement.

For the first time he looks slightly shifty.

"I'm not really supposed to tell anyone that…"

"Who is it?" I ask more forcefully.

"His name's Hannis Baumgartner, said he used to know her."

I nod slowly. "Does he ever visit?"

"No, not once."

I smile. "Thank you for your time."

As I leave the dingy old house, I am incredibly grateful to be returning to my family, to the farm. This has been all the closure I have needed. I can finally shake off these shadows and look forward to the rest of a quiet, simple life with people I actually love.

* * *

That has not yet happened to her. That is a glimpse of the future. I should not read on, now I am clearly in unstable territory. Get rid of the book.

* * *

This is where I end the Mangos montage. I know that it is abrupt since I do not know how some of them died, but I prefer it this way. I find that to know how someone died can alter your view of them. For example, if someone dies in a war you begin to assume they were a hero, selfless, someone who deserves your respect, and this does not necessarily reflect them at all. The truth is that these are the moments I work for; I love every one of these people at some point and the fact that at certain moments I am in awe of them, would advise people to strive to be more like them. I see how they stand out in their vivacity. Yet, at other points you could pass them by as you would people on the street and never know that once they could have captured your heart.

But every one of them lived unashamedly, affected people for better or for worse, and that is why I love watching them. The next set of memories do not directly follow, although do continue the lineage and branch off.

* * *

I scan down the page. My family's names are all there: Sarah, Will, Phoebe and Lisa. There are also other names I do not recognize, people I have not yet met. It must be enough to have this life and to have known the lives of those before and let the future be written as it happens.

Before I can let anything else cloud my judgement, I leap up and drop the book into the open flames, watching the words mar and vanish and the binding slowly crumble. And I relax, I smile. I can keep what I know with me and not be tempted now by the unknown.

Sarah comes back in and sees the roaring fire.

"It's going well!' she exclaims, and I hug her close and kiss her forehead.

She laughs. "By the way, your computer just buzzed in the kitchen. I think you have a new email message."

I wander in, feeling light, and calmly check it. A file springs open holding an elaborate CONGRATULATIONS. It looks as if my fresh start is about to begin.

"I got it!" I yell.

We look through the email together.

"They're pretty vague on descriptions," she notes.

They ask me to come in for further briefing.

"Bloody hell!" she exclaims suddenly. "Look at how much they're paying you!"

We stare at the long figure, dumbstruck.

"What the hell?"

"If you actually have got this, I would never have to work again!" She stares at me and then we both start to laugh.

I arrive back at that makeshift wooden structure and, to my great surprise, I open the doors to a round of applause. I smile nervously at the welcome and then Billy sits me down in his office, beaming at me.

"Well done, son," he says.

I am overwhelmed by this reaction and slightly chuffed at the reception, but my smile doesn't last long as he adds, "We all clapped when you burnt it."

I stare at him. "Sorry?"

"Everyone here wanted you to be chosen out of the ten and you passed." He chuckles.

I stare at him questioningly. "Burnt what?"

He raises his eyebrows, chastising. "The book of course."

There is a loaded silence. Adrenaline spikes through my veins.

"Who are you people? Have you been watching my house?" I get up, heading straight for the door. "Keep my family out of this!"

"Sit down, Will."

"Don't call me Will." I'm pulling on the door but it won't open. "Let me go!"

"We will keep your family out of this and yes, we have been watching you. Now, let's chat."

I stare at him in disbelief. "Who are you? What gives you right to do that?"

"I'm really no one. I'm just a worker and we are not here to discuss rights. The point is that the job is yours if you want it."

I laugh coldly. "What is the job?"

"The book was your interview. We chose to present Sarah and her family's lives to you as we thought that link to you would help you to understand the relevance of this position. And if you do choose to take it on," he laughs amiably, "well, it's almost like you've already read the manual!"

I am lost and he pauses, seeming to realize this. "The key is that you did not read on, but you did feel compelled to finish the lives you'd already started. To us this shows someone who values human life and whose patience can outweigh the need for answers or a story. Critical traits. The powers that be have spoken and the question now remains: William Tief, on the day you die, will you be willing to take over collecting the minutes."

I stare at him. "This position is for when I die?" I ask in shock.

"Indeed, I know this must be slightly baffling and we will give you time to think it over. The contract is for a hundred years and then you are free to pass on in to whoever comes next... as the current collector can do, if you choose to accept."

"This is..." I falter, "a joke?"

"I know you may be having doubts, but let me assure you they had a very elaborate selection process. They do not get their choices wrong. Your love of art and of a story were just the starting point in the choice."

The possibility of this being a reality is slowly seeping into me.

"Will, how else could we have known personal thoughts from your life, or events that had not yet been experienced by your wife?" he says sincerely, seeing my slow and eerily calm acceptance. I feel as if I always knew the book was some sort of test and, when I was reading, I had taken the place of the collector frequently. I nod slowly. "What would be the arrangements up until I 'take' the job?"

"We would pay you handsomely. I believe you have already seen the figure?"

"That's for real? Up front?"

"It is in our interest that you enjoy the rest of your life with your family. A happy man will be better at his job." He smiles ruefully.

The details are discussed endlessly and the only thing left shrouded in mystery at the end of the conversation are the 'hows'. Although I try my luck with prising information about the set-up, this is clearly not for me to know, and so I focus on the facts. By that same evening I have accepted the position.

I wander back to the car in a slight daze, but as I try and digest recent events, I realize that I have never been this happy. Although I cannot explain the situation to anybody, I get to go home and tell my wonderful wife that we are free. Hell, why don't we just up sticks and travel the world. The kids are young enough that we could do that. God, all the things we want to do are now at our finger tips!

I jump into the air spontaneously, the energy needing to go somewhere.

Driving home I also begin to revel in the job that I will do and I realize I couldn't have found a better fit. I have always been a story collector, and I know that I will take pride and enjoyment in what I do. My mind begins to think of all the seven minutes I will be privy too, all the people I will grow to know and understand.

One day, who knows when, I will be coming for your seven minutes. Please make it worth watching.

Special Thanks to two wonderful people without whom I could not have published this book:

Firstly Stephanie Dagg for her editing expertise and insight and Grace Anthony for the beautiful cover design I am much indebted to both of them.

JAY STRITCH

Is a young author from London, England currently studying at Cambridge University.

Having always had a preference for fantasy worlds over the real world it was inevitable that this would manifest itself as a book one day and here are the fruits of many a day dreaming escape from reality.

In her free time she has one too many cats to look after and is a self confessed adrenaline junkie.

Made in the USA
Charleston, SC
16 March 2014